mirrored deception

OTHER BOOKS BY EMMA LEIGH REED

Making the Rules
Breaking the Rules
A Fine Line
A Time to Heal
Second Chances
Trusting Love
Mirrrored Deception

ALSO IN THE MEMORIES OF MURDER SERIES

Hatchet
Spikes

EMMA LEIGH REED

mirrored deception

ELRpublishing

This book is a work of fiction. Names, characters, events, places and incidents are either products of the author's imagination or are used in a fictitious manner. Any resemblance to actual persons, living or dead, or actual events is purely coincidental.

Text copyright © 2022 by Emma Leigh Reed

All rights reserved.

No part of this book may be reproduced, or stored in a retrieval system, or transmitted in any form or by any means, electronic, mechanical, photocopying, recording, or otherwise, without express written permission from the author.

Published by ELR Publishing.
'ISBN-13: 978-1-944550-17-2

Cover and interior design by Kenny Holcomb

Printed in the United States of America

mirrored deception

one

"I will not hire a bodyguard!" Jayla stormed across the room. She righted a small bookshelf and started picking up the books from the floor. "You're overreacting once again." She couldn't believe her sister would even suggest such a thing.

"How can you say that?" Jenna's eyes moved over the mess as she raked her fingers through her hair. "Your apartment has been broken into and trashed. You're being impossible. What do you think Mom and Dad would want you to do if they were here?"

"That's a completely unfair question." Jayla closed her eyes and took a deep breath. Jenna had a way of hitting below the belt using their parents to create guilt, knowing only too well it worked every time.

Jayla grabbed the broom from the living room closet to sweep up the broken shards of glass from pictures that had been scattered about the room. "I'll think about it, okay?" she whispered, only wanting to make peace with her twin.

"You know I love you, Jayla. I just don't want anything to happen to you." Jenna's voice softened. "I worry about you."

"I know, but you really don't have to. I don't think he'll bother me again." Jayla's voice broke. She wished she could show more confidence and put her sister at ease. Jayla studied the concern in her eyes, and it was like looking into a mirror. They were identical twins, yet very different.

"I've got to go, Sis. Will you be okay?"

"Of course, Jen. I'm fine. I'll just clean up." Jayla walked her to the door and hugged her close. "I love you. Please don't worry."

As she shut the door and turned to survey the damage—the overturned chair and knick-knacks scattered about the living room—Jayla choked back tears. How could he have done this to her? The pictures of her family were broken and strewn about the floor.

She didn't need a bodyguard. She just needed to get away from it all. Every *bit* of it.

She headed to the bedroom, dragged a couple of suitcases out of the closet, and started throwing clothes into them. Should she tell Jenna she was leaving?

No.

Jayla wanted to disappear and give herself a chance to think. Jenna would only tell her she couldn't run from her problems and needed to meet them head on.

Jayla needed something more than that. She slammed the suitcases shut, grabbed her laptop, and headed outdoors. She threw the bags in the trunk of her car and gave a good look around the parking lot. Convinced no one was around, she jumped in and started the engine. She pulled her hair back in an elastic band and drove off. With no destination in mind, she aimed for the coast.

For the first few miles, she kept a watchful eye out for anyone following. After an hour, it became clear she was the only one on the road. Her grip loosened on the steering wheel, the tension leaving her shoulders. She rolled the windows down to smell the cool ocean breeze, and her mind wandered.

She wanted her life back. Yet, she wanted a *different* life. Lately, regrets consumed her.

The curving coastal route kept her focus, and she paid no attention to the time until her stomach grumbled, reminding her she'd missed dinner. Then she became *very* aware of the time. Dark shadows had crept across the landscape.

She clicked on the headlights, and her eyes were drawn to the gas gauge. *Empty.* How could she take off on a whim without thinking of fueling up? She could hear levelheaded Jenna now—"You're *never* thinking."

At a bend in the road, the headlights illuminated a sign for a bed-and-breakfast, The Cliffhouse, with a posting below it for vacancies. Jayla perked up a bit. At least it wasn't far ahead, and it would do for the night.

She turned into the entrance and drove up the winding, cobblestone driveway. Around the last turn, a large Victorian house came into view. The place was dark. Not surprising since it was ten o'clock. Hopefully, someone was still up.

Jayla sat for a moment and wondered if they were open. The needle on the gas gauge hovered just at empty; she had no choice but see if they had a room for the night.

She grabbed her small overnight bag and left the rest of the luggage in the car. After locking the car doors, she walked briskly up the steps of the veranda, past the wicker furniture. In the dark, Jayla rang the bell and waited. She shivered, straining to see beyond the porch. Seconds ticked by, so she wrapped her arms around her middle and paced in front of the door.

The hairs on the back of her neck tingled with the sense of being watched. But that couldn't be. The place was out in the middle of nowhere. She shook off the sensation—just remnants of the god-awful day.

Her impatience surged, and she rapped harder on the door.

"Yes, I'm coming!" a male voice sounded from inside.

The door swung open. *Finally.*

She was about to speak, but when she got her

first look at him, words couldn't get past her lips.

The man filling the door leaned nonchalantly against the doorjamb and studied her. His tousled dark hair looked as if he'd just gotten out of bed. His tanned, bare chest had her pulse racing. "Yes?"

That single word brought a sizzle of awareness coursing through her body. "I'm...er...sorry. I didn't realize the time, and I was running out of gas."

He glanced over her shoulder to the car and back again. Perfectly shaped eyebrows rose while sensuous brown eyes surveyed her from head to toe. Okay, she probably didn't look too presentable after the long road trip. The salty air had given her skin that needs-to-be washed feel. Forget about the lipstick, which had undoubtedly been gone for hours.

His scrutiny made her uneasy. Surely, he could say more than one word?

Jayla shoved a lock of hair behind her ear. "Do you have a room available?"

He stood upright, away from the doorframe, without saying a thing. Jayla couldn't help but notice how his well-worn jeans looked like they'd been hastily zipped up, the tab partially undone.

"Come in." He stepped aside.

She followed. The foyer was small, but well kept.

He stopped at a desk and turned. "How long are you staying?"

"Tonight, maybe longer." Jayla tried to read him. He didn't invite small talk. "I'm Jayla, Jayla Ralston."

"Okay, Jayla." He said her name slowly, almost seductively. "Sign here. Name's Tristan."

She nodded and leaned down to complete the paperwork, then looked up and met his dark brown eyes. Her pulse ratcheted up another beat. Something in his sharp look held her gaze.

He finally broke the spell and gestured for her to follow him to her room. "If you need anything, I'll be around in the morning."

She let out a deep breath. The place might do after all. No one would look for her there.

Alone at last.

She dug out her laptop and started to write.

The change was just beginning.

Trenton watched until after midnight when the house had finally gotten dark. Only one guest had checked in tonight. The only light left on was the one on the veranda.

He slipped around to the west side of the building, treading carefully on the pebbled walkway, not wanting to leave any footprints. He'd watched the house for months and knew the west side wing was empty and that there didn't appear to be plans to fill the rooms even in the busy months of the summer. At the side door that once was the servant's entrance, he ran his hand along the top of the doorframe and found the key put there years ago. Sixteen years, to be exact.

He chuckled. The poor fool probably forgot it was there, or forgot anyone else knew about it. The key slid easily into the lock. It still worked. He let himself in, shut the door, and waited for his eyes to adjust to the dark. Though it didn't matter. The place was as familiar as the back of his hand.

He pocketed the key and started for the back stairs, carrying one bag that held all his current belongings. He had come back to claim what was rightfully his, and claim it he would, not matter how long it took to get it.

Halfway up the stairs, he stopped and listened. There were no sounds, other than his own breathing. He shook his head and continued up to the first bedroom. Trenton lay on the bed fully clothed, eyes closed. He couldn't let his memory play tricks on him. They were gone. He had survived. He was back—and would make sure certain people paid for what he had been through.

Two

Trenton awoke, stiff and cold. He was groggy, but as he looked around, he remembered arriving just a few short hours ago. Outside, the ocean crashed on the rocks, and the seagulls called for their breakfast. For a brief moment, he allowed himself the luxury of remembering a happier time…of being a young boy who enjoyed those sounds, as he ran through the halls of the house.

He listened intently for any noises that would indicate he wasn't alone. With a groan, he stood and shook off the memories. He dug his razor and shaving cream out of his bag. Facing the bathroom mirror, he stared at the reflection. Features he no longer recognized looked back at him. The jet-black hair had gotten long and was in need of a haircut. The square chin covered with three-day's growth of beard. The eyes had long ago lost their sparkle and love for life.

He scowled and started shaving. Once finished, he ran his hand over the now-smooth angle of the jaw. It would do for now.

Trenton moved to the window, and drew back the curtain to look out. The sun danced liked diamonds off the waves. He curled his lips into a smile and allowed his shoulders to relax. He was home.

Home.

He took in the rock wall at the edge of the trees as he leaned against the window. The memories flooded back. His heart quickened as he recalled running along the rock wall playing tag with his brother and laughing, and his father calling out to them to be careful as he laughed with them. Trenton sighed. He'd been happier then.

Those were days long gone, and the reasons for his return jolted him out of nostalgia. The hatred hit him hard, and his insides turned to ice. There were plans to be made.

Wary of the daylight, he made his way across the brief stretch of lawn to the dense woods. He found the worn path—now overgrown with brush—and made his way toward the family carriage house. How many years had it sat empty? The old man had died—Trenton had read it in the paper nearly ten years ago. It had been kept quiet since some ruled it as a suicide.

Trenton had gone to the funeral and stayed in

the back, well hidden. He'd expected to see her there, but she was conspicuously absent. The other one had been there, looking sad. He had overheard the owner of the bed-and-breakfast say he was alone now. "No family left." Where had she gone? He must find out. The carriage house would hold the answers, if there were any to be found.

As the woods cleared, the carriage house came into view. He assumed no one used it anymore, and certainly, no one had been there in years. The very reason that he had parked his motorcycle out in front of it and covered it with a tarp. He knew no one would see it parked there.

He pushed open the door and stepped inside, instantly feeling his dad's presence beside him. The answers had to lie within those walls. His dad's death wasn't suicide, yet it had been ruled as one. He'd died when Trenton was nine, and it wasn't right to have parents taken at that age. Trenton knew the old man had done it, and a year after the *suicide*, at the age of ten, Trenton confronted him. The old man hit him right across the face and told him never to speak of it again. Trenton had no idea at that time that he would pay for it; pay with his *soul* for many years to come. He had lost so much.

He shook his head and glanced around. The dust had built up over the years and lay like thick grime over the windows. It covered the furniture that was still here. He flipped the light switch and was relieved the electricity was on. Upstairs had been his dad's study. He would start there.

He mounted the stairs slowly. There was no one there, yet the place felt cold in spite of the warmth of the June sun. A shiver ran down his spine. Was that supposed to be a message? His senses had always been trustworthy, but all of a sudden Trenton felt like an intruder.

Something crackled outside. Leaves? Or footsteps? He stopped, listening carefully. He shook his head. Just his imagination. The old man would not be an albatross any longer. Trenton was there for one reason and one reason only…

Revenge.

Jayla awoke to the sounds of the ocean. She gazed around the room, familiarizing herself with the surroundings. It was a small room, but homey. An overstuffed chair sat in the corner, facing the large window. Next to it was a small table where she'd set her laptop late the night before when she finally stopped writing.

The realization of what she had done—taken off without saying a word to anyone—hit her. *Freed* her. She pushed the thoughts of Jenna's impending worry from her mind.

She stretched, got up, and crossed the room to pull back the curtain from the window. Her breath caught at the view. The blue-green ocean seemed endless, running into the cloudless sky. Jayla smiled and drew herself away to look over the grounds.

Along the cliff, a dirt walkway wandered as far as the eye could see. A sense of urgency to explore came over her, and she rushed to get dressed.

Momentarily, she forgot about her apartment—and even Jenna. Jayla felt pulled back to her younger years when she and Jenna explored places with just their imaginations.

She headed down the stairs, following the exotic aroma of fresh-baked cinnamon rolls all the way to the dining room. A sideboard contained a basket of rolls and a carafe of coffee. The rumble of her stomach reminded her she had skipped dinner.

"Help yourself." A deep voice from behind startled her.

Jayla turned to find Tristan watching, a smile playing on his lips.

"Thanks." She crossed the room, poured a cup of coffee, and helped herself to a roll, hoping her facial expression remained neutral. Void of the excitement at seeing Tristan.

He had looked handsome last night, although standoffish. Today, her knees got weak just looking at his smile. She could not forget the reason why she *got away from it all* to begin with her ex-roommate who wanted more than she did—and who had childishly trashed her apartment when he was asked to leave.

She settled in a chair close to the window and watched the ocean, mesmerized.

"It's beautiful, isn't it?" Tristan startled her again, and she nearly spilled her coffee. She didn't realize he'd joined her.

"Yes." She played with the coffee cup, not making eye contact.

"So, what's your story, Jayla?" He leaned back, his eyes roaming over her.

In a hurry to leave the bedroom, she hadn't put on any makeup and had pulled her long, brown hair into a simple ponytail.

"Vacation? Meeting someone?"

"No story. Just here for a little R and R." Jayla rose quickly. "I think I'll go enjoy the walk along the cliff." She picked up her roll and hurried to the door, heart racing. Could he see through her and know she was running?

Out on the veranda, she drew in the salty air. The seagulls called *good morning* as she started out. She spied a stone path and walked along it as it led around the house and came to a crossway. She could either go on to the cliff walk or follow a branch off the path through a wrought-iron arbor overloaded with red roses. She closed her eyes and inhaled the sweet scent. Without a doubt, she'd found the perfect place to relax.

She turned right, followed the path, and passed through the rose-covered arbor, entering another world. One filled with roses. Surrounded by a hedge, the garden was completely secluded. A bench sat in the back corner. To the right of the bench, a yellow rose bush in full bloom called to her. She approached it and delicately touched the blossoms.

"That one was my mother's favorite."

Jayla turned to find Tristan wandering around

the roses, stopping every so often to smell one. Her stomach clenched with anxiety. She didn't want someone always a step behind.

"They're beautiful." She crossed and sat on the bench. "I could sit for hours in here."

"That's exactly what my mom said too, and she would." He sounded thoughtful. "She came here when she had a lot on her mind, or needed to get away from the stress. I guess I keep it open for the guests, hoping they can find peace here, too."

"I'm glad. I love it already."

"I'll let you get back to your walk. If you need anything, just let me know." He gave her a thoughtful glance before heading toward the arbored entrance.

Jayla admired the well-fitted jeans as he left the garden. Her face warmed. She wasn't there to admire the manly view. She'd had enough man-trouble to last a while.

She sighed. Maybe the walk would clear her head. Something about Tristan's presence clouded her thinking.

It was secluded there in general, even more so than the rose garden. The well-manicured lawns extended to the cliff overlooking the ocean. To the right of the lawn were rocks, to the left a dense wooded area. She reached the cliff, stopped, and stared. The drop-off went straight down to jagged rocks below.

She rapidly stepped back. Her heart quickened a beat.

I hate heights…

She moved onto the dirt path and headed toward the wooded area. The walkway ended at the edge of the woods. There were steps carved into the rocks, steps that led to *nothing*.

Jayla shrugged and turned back for the house. She decided to stay a while, liking the seclusion. No one would track her there.

She found Tristan at the front desk in the foyer and arranged to stay for three weeks. His eyes showed open curiosity, but he held his tongue. She offered no explanations.

With a quick smile of thanks, she went to grab her laptop and retired to the rose garden. She welcomed the opportunity to continue to find herself. Soon, she was lost in another world. One she didn't relish leaving for a long time.

Jayla shivered. She pulled herself away from the computer and realized the sun was riding low in the sky. Losing-herself was becoming a habit. She saved everything before shutting down the laptop, then stretched as she stood.

What a peaceful spot.

Finally free to do what she wanted, she longed to stay there forever, never returning home or to reality. Jenna would be having a fit about now with the realization that Jayla was gone. A twang of guilt sliced through her, but she just couldn't bring herself to call.

She picked up the laptop and headed for the house. Jayla rounded the front of the building, but slowed when she saw Tristan sitting on the veranda, staring into space. She didn't want to interrupt and slowed her pace to a stop, uncertain what to do.

"Come on up. You're not bothering me." His voice was low, and his eyes never turned toward her.

She cautiously walked up the stairs. "I didn't want to disturb you. You looked deep in thought."

"Just a lot on my mind, I guess." Tristan gestured toward the chair next to him. "Care to join me?"

"Sure." Jayla sat and played with the cover of the laptop.

"Been writing?"

"Yes." Jayla smiled. "I totally lost track of time."

"What's it about?"

"Oh, it's a children's story. Probably nothing you'd be interested in." She dropped her glance to her lap and fear gripped her from out of nowhere. Her chest tightened in panic, and she rose to her feet. "I need to get inside."

"No rush. I'd love to hear about your story." Tristan stood next to her and rested his hand on her arm. The heat from his touch warmed her. "Don't go in yet."

She searched his eyes. "I can't stay. I need to make a call. Sorry."

Jayla hurried inside, the panic gradually lessening. Why was she afraid to talk about the book? Likely because she felt Jenna would disapprove. Jayla longed for encouragement that she could be a good writer. Yet she also needed the freedom to do it without anyone knowing. Then she could fail, and no one would be the wiser. Fear of continually failing, while her twin sister succeeded in everything, ripped away any confidence Jayla had years ago.

She was a good schoolteacher, but that was easy since it was a *noble profession*—according to Jenna.

Jayla sighed. How different would life be if she could just get out from under her sister? She hated that thought. She loved Jenna and didn't want to lose her. So much had already been lost in her life—which ironically was the very reason she permitted her sister to continually suffocate her.

She shut her door and leaned against it. With her eyes closed, she tried to remember her parents. Over the past few years, the memories had faded. Had they encouraged her to do things? Had they always favored Jenna? Jayla tried and tried, but couldn't conjure a single memory. Only hurt and pain radiated through her.

She pushed away from the door, dropped the laptop on the bed, and moved toward the window. The sight of the ocean always calmed her nerves. She needed this. She tried to envision what it would be like living there full time, raising a family close to the crashing waves.

She shook her head to free it from those thoughts as she stared out at the view. Her life was being a school teacher of young children. *Those* children would always be her family. She just couldn't imagine ever having a love so true that she would settle down and be married with a family of her own.

Three

Jayla settled into the routine of the bed-and-breakfast life. She enjoyed the short drive to a quaint small town not too far for shopping and other meals. She relaxed with long walks on the beach and sat for hours in the rose garden, writing. Oddly enough, it felt like she had found her home. In her relaxed state of mind, her writing drew her in, causing time to stand still. The words flew across the screen. Her surroundings became a blur until she looked up, sometimes to find Tristan watching.

She headed to the rose garden early Friday morning to find Tristan already there, weeding. She hesitated at the entryway as his arms flexed with every movement, showing the chiseled muscles of his arms.

"Come on in," he said. "I hope I won't disturb your writing. Just wanted to finish up here. I've been trying to do it in between your visits." Tristan leaned back on his haunches. He was in shorts and his tank top lay on the ground beside him. His muscular arms glistened with the sweat of his work.

"I can c-come back," Jayla stammered, realizing she was staring.

"Not necessary. I don't mind you working in here while I finish up, as long as I'm not disturbing you." He smiled and brushed off a trickle of sweat running down his forehead.

"Of course not. It's your garden." She started for the bench. As he bent over the flowerbed, Jayla admired his smooth, tanned back. The muscles flexed with every weed he pulled, and she inwardly groaned. How would she get any writing done with him in front of her like that? She had been escaping to the rose garden to avoid him!

She opened the laptop and brought up her children's story. Rereading it, Jayla let her mind wander as Tristan pulled weeds and worked the ground around the roses, adding fertilizer to the soil.

"Did you work out here with your mother when you were a child?" she asked.

"No. She had a gardener. I helped him occasionally, but I learned to do this on my own after she was…gone."

Jayla wondered why the pause all of a sudden, and speculated that he must miss her still. "How long has she been gone?"

"Long enough." He quickly rose. "Well, looks like this is done. I'll leave you alone now." He stared at her for a minute. "You're welcome to eat dinner here at The Cliffhouse tonight instead of going off into town."

"I didn't know you offered dinner, too," Jayla said in surprise.

"Well, I mean…would you like to have dinner here with me tonight? I grill a mean steak." He grinned, eyebrows raised.

Jayla laughed. "Yeah, I'd like that."

"Great. Say, sixish?"

She nodded. "See you then." Her fingers tapped against her laptop.

Did she need to avoid him? Tristan was very good-looking and obviously family oriented. What would one dinner hurt? She'd been there a week already, and he hadn't made any advances toward her. She had two more weeks that were paid for before she was considering moving on.

Hmm…

She would see what happened.

Jayla parked her car in town and got out to walk. On a previous trip, she had found a cute little shop that sold sundresses.

A new dress might be just the thing for tonight's dinner with Tristan.

She stopped short on the sidewalk. Two stores

down, Tristan stood, looking in a store window. She could have sworn he was at The Cliffhouse before she left.

Yes, he'd been sweeping the front porch.

"Tristan? What a surprise." She approached him.

He turned to her and smiled. "Hello there."

"I didn't expect to see you here in town. I thought you were busy at The Cliffhouse when I left." Jayla searched his face until their eyes met. There was something different, a sadness she didn't see earlier.

"Just had to run out for a few things and need to get back. I'll see you back there." He smiled, leaned forward, and kissed her on the cheek, then headed off down the street. "Have fun!" he called over his shoulder. He seemed more like himself, and she shrugged off her earlier feelings.

Jayla turned and stared after him. Her mind cleared of all thoughts. She suddenly giggled to herself and made a beeline for the dress shop. She knew exactly what she wanted to wear tonight.

It would be a night for revelations and surprises.

She entered the dress shop and browsed the sundresses. She found a causal one that complemented her figure, so she tried it on. It fit perfectly. Satisfied, she smiled. It had been a long time since she felt the excitement of having dinner with a man. Her stomach clenched in anticipation of the night. In the past week, she had been able to relax and forget the last few months of trouble she had experienced with Ryan. She felt freer than she had in years.

After paying for the dress, Jayla headed outside

with a spring in her step. She stopped and regarded her reflection in the big, plate-glass window. Her skin was clear, it needed no makeup. Her blue eyes sparkled with anticipation of the upcoming night. Maybe just a hint of mascara would be all that she'd do for makeup tonight.

Her stomach fluttered with the butterflies inside as she dressed for dinner. The new, sky-blue sundress highlighted her eyes, and it had a high waist and a V-neck, buttoned top. A pair of woven sandals finished the outfit. She applied black mascara lightly to her eyelashes and stepped back to survey the results. Pleased with her appearance, she gave a twirl and curtsied at the reflection in the mirror.

Jayla skipped down the stairs and paused at the entrance to the dining room. Her stomach fluttered with nervousness. An accompanying wave of apprehension swept through, too. She flashed back to Tristan's shy behavior over the past week, and then his more intriguing side in town today. That was the man she suddenly wanted to know more about. Which man would be there tonight? She would take her cues from him, but how she hoped it wasn't the *shy, stumbling-over-his words Tristan.* She smiled to herself.

She pushed open the door to the dining room. He had his back to her, bent over a little, and carefully setting the table. She admired his jeans with a simple light blue jersey tucked in as he placed the silverware beside the plates. A single rose in the middle of the table lent an intimate, yet simple look.

"It looks lovely." Jayla entered.

Tristan stood upright, turned, and faced her. "Thank you, as do you." He smiled and pulled out a chair for her.

"Did you do all this?" Jayla gestured to the rose on the table, and the vases of even more roses around the dining room.

"Yes. It's nothing really. I know you enjoy the rose garden. I thought you might enjoy the smell of them in here also."

"I do. They're gorgeous. It must have taken some time to pick them though."

Tristan shrugged, noncommittal, as he moved to the sideboard to get the salads. Jayla watched him, trying to figure out where the evening would lead. He was being shy and quiet, and she wondered where the *outgoing Tristan* had gone.

"What was it like growing up here?" Jayla tried to break the ice.

His face lit up. "I loved it. As kids, Trent and I were constantly outside."

"Trent?"

"He was my twin brother. He died when we were ten."

"Oh, I'm so sorry, Tristan. I had no idea."

"It's okay. I have very fond memories of him. There isn't a day that goes by that I don't think of him. I'm not quite sure what happened. I just remember my mother telling me they had taken him to the doctor's in the night, and he had died. I was young and really broken up over it. I didn't come out of our room for days." He toyed with his salad; his eyes distant, taken back with his memory. "We had so many good times, playing out on the cliff rocks, through the woods. We spent a lot of time at the carriage house with my dad while he painted."

Jayla smiled. "I know what it's like to have a connection with a twin, because I am one. It's something special and very different than just another sibling."

"Definitely, and you can't explain it to other people. You don't get it unless you're a twin yourself." He grinned. "There are days I wonder what it would be like if Trent was still around and we were running this place together. Still getting into trouble, I'm sure. Trenton was always more eager to try things out. I was a bit more cautious. Yet, I always followed behind him."

"Sounds a lot like me and Jenna. She was the more adventurous one, yet I always followed behind." Jayla laughed. "And got in more trouble."

They continued to talk about their childhoods through dinner. The atmosphere relaxed. Jayla found herself at ease and opened up to Tristan about lifelong dreams of writing a children's book. "Jenna never would understand, so all these years I've never done it. Staying here has given me a chance to make some changes in my life, including starting this book I always wanted to write."

"I think it's great. You need to follow your heart and dreams." Tristan cleared the table and started for the kitchen. "I'll be right back with some coffee and dessert."

Jayla got up and wandered, stopping to smell the roses around the room. She felt a kinship with Tristan tonight, yet the excitement at seeing him that afternoon and having him kiss her was gone. Something seemed different about him tonight that she just couldn't put her finger on.

"Cheesecake?" His voice rolled the word, sounding almost seductive. Jayla stared at him for a moment. Maybe he wasn't so different after all.

"Absolutely."

"Why don't we take this into the living room? I started the fireplace."

"Sounds wonderful." Jayla picked up the coffee cups and followed him. Who was this man in front of her? A man full of secrets.

Trenton watched from behind the tapestry.

Years ago as a child, he ran through the house using the secret passages and knew them like the back of his hand. Each room had a tapestry covering a secret door. He took in the conversation between Tristan and Jayla and narrowed his eyes as he listened to Tristan reminisce. His body warmed with anger, and it was all he could do to stay quiet. He wanted to go and confront his brother and tell him that was not how it had been.

He listened to Jayla talk about her dreams of writing, and he softened. She mentioned always being in the shadow of her sister, and he sympathized.

At that moment, he knew he needed to get to know her more. How, he wasn't sure, but he felt a strong pull to her, a definite connection he had never felt so instantaneously with any other woman before.

He slipped back into the passage and moved to the west wing to mull over his next move. Things would have to change.

four

The heat warmed Jayla's face and the sun shone in her eyes as she struggled awake. She rolled onto her back and stared out the window at the clouds moving gently across the sky. She couldn't stop thinking of the night before. Tristan had been such a gentleman, and she enjoyed the evening without a doubt. She had shared her innermost dreams with the man, something she had never done before.

With a sigh, she sat up and got out of bed. Her feet hit the cold, wood floor and a chill ran through her. She grabbed her robe and rushed to the shower. The warm water raining over her took away the chills as she allowed her mind to focus on her book. She was so engrossed in mentally writing the plot, she lost track of time. The water soon cooled. She didn't want to lose the plot in her thoughts, so she dried quickly, threw on shorts and a tank top, then grabbed her laptop and headed for the rose garden. Thankful not to run into Tristan, she immediately started writing.

So intrigued in the story, the sound of the distant footsteps startled her from her thoughts.

"I'm sorry, I didn't mean to startle you." Tristan, clad in khakis and a short-sleeved T-shirt, walked toward her. "You looked so focused, I didn't want to interrupt. But you're so beautiful in the sunlight, I couldn't resist joining you."

"It's okay. I'm at a point where I can take a break." Jayla saved the changes and closed her laptop. "I enjoyed last night."

"Me too."

She glanced up and her eyes met his. They were intense and dark, and Jayla found herself unable to look away. Her stomach knotted with excitement. The feeling of intrigue came over her, and she wondered at this different side of Tristan once again.

"Tell me, Tristan, how do you manage to run this place and find time to watch me write?" She moved restlessly on the bench, feeling the pull from his gaze. She needed to break his hold, so she turned to the roses.

His chuckle made her feel like a giddy teenager. "You, my dear, have a way of taking me away from my chores, I'm afraid. Do I disturb you?"

"No." She stood and went to smell a nearby rose.

MIRRORED DECEPTION

Her hand trembled as she reached for it.

"One of my favorites." He was beside her; his hand covered hers as she touched the delicate petals.

"I-- it's mine also. I love the yellow ones." Her voiced wavered, and she cleared it.

"They suit you much more than the red. Personally, I think this one over here, the lavender-blue, matches your eyes." He kept hold of her hand and led her to the back corner where he showed her a small bush she hadn't really paid much attention to before. "It's a subtle color and not many people seem to notice it."

"It's beautiful." Jayla bent to smell it. "So fragrant."

"Much like yourself." He lifted her hand to his lips and pressed a kiss to the back of her fingers. "I must leave you, though. Until later, Jayla. Enjoy your writing."

She stood next to the lavender-blue rose, watching him leave the garden. Who was this man? Quiet and shy one minute, bold and full of charm the next. She gazed at her fingers—recalling his tender kiss—and smiled. Yes, this was the man who brought excitement—ignited a burning inside her that called for more. She *needed* more of him.

Trenton slipped around the back of the house to the worn path, blending into the shadows. He smiled as he thought back to the brief encounter with Jayla.

A tightening in his stomach had him wondering just what it would be like to hold her close. He shook his head and started again for the carriage house. He had to be careful not to seek her out too often in daylight.

His mind wandered to his brother. Anger filled him. All those years, being held captive, waiting for him to show up. Where was the twin intuition all that time? Did Tristan not *want* to find him? Trent highly doubted their mother would lie about him dying. His mother had loved him.

Trenton went into the carriage house and started for the basement. There had to be answers somewhere in that place. He would find them even if he had to tear apart every inch of it.

He shivered as he crept down the stairs. Coldness surrounded him, and he stopped halfway down, gripped with fear. How many times over the past years had he stayed out of dark and damp places just to avoid being afraid? He was stronger than that, but he froze in place. He mentally shook off the fear and took another step down. Shadows played tricks on his eyes, and he forced himself to continue. He looked for the light pull cord. His muscles strained from the tension. Eerie quietness encased him, and he pulled the cord. Light flooded the basement, and the shadows instantly disappeared.

From the middle of the room, Trenton slowly turned in a circle, searching for the best place to start looking. Several boxes were stacked in the far corner. He moved toward them. This the decisive moment he had been looking for.

He placed his hands on the top one and stopped. Did he really want the truth? The anger was easier to live with. What if things were not how he envisioned them all these years? He closed his eyes and let the bitterness envelop him. This was his home. He had just as much right to it as Tristan, yet his brother was running it alone.

Trenton ripped into the first box. He found it filled with old letters and threw it aside to open the next one. Photo albums. He paused long enough to open one and see a family picture of when he and Tristan were about three. Each parent held one boy. Happiness cut through his hardened heart, only to be replaced with bitterness that his father had been taken from him, *brutally*.

He shoved aside box after box, working his way through half of them before he abruptly stopped. The current box held his mother's clothes. He lifted out one of the blouses and brought it to his face. He rubbed it against his cheek, longing for her to be there. How could she have just let him go? He closed his eyes, memories flooding him. She had always favored Tristan, and Trent had been closer to their dad. Regardless, he believed their mother had enough love for both twins.

Trent threw the garment back in the box. He moved the clothes from side to side, searching for a clue as to what had happened to her. Nothing but clothes. The need to have answers overcame him with fury. He tossed boxes in anger and frustration. Time had passed quickly in his search.

He peered around as he moved to the back of the basement. Nothing. Nothing in sight. He needed to find *something*.

He paused at the sound of the howling wind coming through the drafty windows. Somewhere in the house above him, the floor creaked as it seemed to respond to the cold outside. He strained his ears to assure himself that he was alone. The years had hardened him and made him leery of trusting any sound.

With a sigh, he started the process of putting boxes back. He had no idea how often Tristan came to the house and didn't want to give away that there had been a visitor. He clicked off the light and went cautiously to the stairs. Listening again, he realized it had begun to rain. Slowly, he ascended to the main floor.

He could either get wet heading back to the west wing, or settle in there for the night. Not a place he relished being. After the barrage of memories over the last hour, sleep would be slow in coming.

He stood in the window of the living room while the rain pelleted the porch. *How often had Tristan sat and watched the rain in the past years?* The early years of sitting with his dad and Trist on the back porch during a storm, watching the sky light up over the ocean, sprang to his mind. He pushed away a nagging in his gut reminding him that there had been good times, and forced his thoughts to Jayla. She pulled at him until his senses were clouded. She had a softness and quality about her that made him feel loved.

Groaning, he turned from the window and started upstairs. He could keep vigil better from the back bedroom that overlooked The Cliffhouse. He wanted to feel Jayla's presence. He swore under his breath, wondering if she was with Tristan.

five

Jayla leaned her head against the cool windowpane. The rain pelted the house, and yet she welcomed the sight of grayness over the ocean. It mirrored her feelings. She couldn't figure out Tristan. Shy and aloof one moment, taking her breath away the next. The moment in the garden had ignited sparks she long felt were gone.

She pushed away from the window, grabbed the laptop, and let her mind wander to the plot. Her creativity flowed and brought her to life, and her hands flew over the keyboard.

A quiet knock pulled her from her thoughts. She shoved the computer aside and moved toward the door. "Yes?"

"It's Tristan. I saw your light and was concerned. Are you okay?"

She glanced at the clock. One-thirty. Where had the time gone? She pulled the door open. "I'm fine. Didn't realize the time."

Tristan met Jayla's eyes. "I happened to be walking by." He slid his gaze downward. The thin top Jayla was wearing melted against her like a second skin.

He quickly looked at her face again and discovered a raised eyebrow and fortunately, a smile.

"I'm sorry for disturbing you," he said. "I was just checking to make sure everything was okay. Good night." He hastily turned and started down the hallway, willing his body not to respond.

"Good night, Tristan," she called after him. "Sleep well." Her door softly clicked shut.

With a sigh of relief, he headed for his room. How could he be so foolish to gawk at her? She wasn't typically his type. The artsy kind never appealed to him, yet he was drawn to something other than her beauty. She had a gentleness that pulled at memories from long ago.

He leaned against the now-closed door, eyes shut, and let every recollection flood over him. His mother had been ripped away from him when he was young. He never fully grasped the implication that she had gone crazy from Trenton's death. All he remembered was her holding him and laughing at Trenton's antics just days before he died. Trenton had always made her laugh. The differences between his brother and him had been subtle, but the biggest was Tristan's soft side and Trenton's desire for constant adventure. Tristan would trail after him, wanting to be part of the fun.

Along with Tristan's desire for adventure, a part of him died the day Trenton left his life. His mother had always brushed off his questions until she finally succumbed to the mental illness that took over her.

Tristan threw himself on the bed and fought to stop the whirlwind of the past in his mind. He always felt that Trenton was still part of him, and he had no closure to his death. The fact of the matter was that Tristan was alone and his family was gone.

With a growl, he stood and crossed to the window. The feeling of comfort quickly passed over him, and just as quickly, the hairs on the back of his neck prickled.

Something was wrong.

Jayla curled up under the covers, wondering why Tristan was so standoffish. Her thoughts wandered to what his lips would feel like against hers. What his hands would feel like as he wrapped them around her waist, pulling her against his lean, hard body.

With a sigh, she rolled over. Sleep would not come easily tonight.

She suddenly missed Jenna and picked up her cell phone to call her. She punched in Jenna's number, but dropped the phone onto the bed before pushing

Send. One-thirty in the morning. Jenna would not be happy to hear from her at that time. Jayla quickly picked it up again and simply typed in a text:

Gone away for a mini-vacation. Need time alone. Talk to you soon.

It would be just one more thing her sister would say she was doing wrong.

Tears seeped out of her eyes. She missed Jenna but felt she couldn't go home quite yet. She needed to get her story out—at least the first draft. She had limited time until the school year started. This was a good break for the summer, though guilt sliced through her at not having told Jen where she was.

Jayla turned away from the clock.

Trenton's arms ached to hold Jayla as he watched her toss and turn, trying to sleep. It was late. He wanted her more than he had wanted any woman.

He shut the door behind the tapestry and turned to the west wing and the overwhelming loneliness. The more he saw her, the emptier he felt.

He moved quietly, cursing his brother. His mind raced over the possibilities of where to go next, the outcomes, and how to protect Jayla from his anger. He needed to get Tristan's attention. Jayla being in the picture brought obstacles he hadn't anticipated. Part of him hoped she wasn't staying long, while the other part couldn't get enough of her.

Six

Jayla stood at the cliff overlooking the ocean. She stared down at the raging dark waves as they crashed along the stones below. This trip had been a great getaway from her troubles at home but also a time of reflection. She knew in her heart she had never dealt with the problems she faced years ago. They still haunted her today.

She tightly wrapped her arms across her chest as the cold wind whipped her hair into her face. She drifted back to three years ago when her world was crashing down around her. Her parents were gone, and relationship after relationship ended in heartache. She ached so badly to be loved, to have someone hold her. At the age of twenty-two, she believed she would never have that. Her parents shared a strong love that ran deep. A marriage that had stood through some tough financial times. Their love for each other never seemed to falter.

Jayla had felt numb after the accident and slipped into the background, letting Jenna take over. Their parents had been gone now for five years, but the pain was still as intense as if it had happened yesterday. The first year was blurry. Jayla continued to finish her teaching degree and started to work while Jenna had gone into selling antiques. She was envious of her sister. She seemed so *put together* all the time while Jayla's life seemed to spiral out of control the following two years after their death.

Jayla shuddered at the thought of the relationships she had thrown herself into, only to be left again and again. She never realized until recently how much she longed for the marriage her parents had, and as a result, had pushed and pushed every guy she dated.

She looked around, disoriented, and shook her head to clear it. Her emotions had been so strong, she had forgotten her surroundings. She peered down at the waves crashing on the rocks. The pounding sound soothed her nerves as the wind kicked up around her. She turned toward the house and ducked as the wind whipped her hair into her face. The rocks along the path tripped her, and she stumbled into something hard. She glanced up into amused eyes and melted into the warmth of the arms that wrapped around her.

"I'm sorry. I didn't see you."

"I gathered since you were looking down." Tristan smirked. "Enjoying the ocean?"

"I was. Guess I lost myself in the soothing sound of it." Jayla pushed out of his arms. Not wanting to be held, but not wanting him to let go. She shivered, suddenly colder without the warmth of his arms.

"I'll let you get to the house then."

She sidestepped him and hurried past with a glance over her shoulder to see him watching her, his face vulnerable for a brief second before becoming uninterested. Who was this man that caused conflicted emotions in her? One moment he was shy, the next, he pulled such intense reactions from her with his touch, his smile, and the warmth in his eyes.

Jayla rushed to the door, stepped inside, and was instantly surrounded by warmth. She leaned against the closed door and breathed a sigh of relief. The turmoil inside her brought too many memories to the surface—memories she would rather forget. She fought hard to remember the good ones: her dad playing with them, her mom's encouragement.

She caught a glimpse of Tristan going into the dining room. Stunned that he beat her inside, she followed. He had his back to her, and she watched him stare out the window. He seemed to be deep in thought, and she didn't want to intrude, so she started to back out of the room.

She froze when the floor creaked and Tristan turned. The sadness on his face mirrored her feelings.

"Sorry," she said. "I didn't want to interrupt you." Jayla gestured to leave.

"Don't go. Come have a cup of coffee. You look half frozen." He moved to the sideboard to pour the coffee, bringing no argument from her.

Jayla met him halfway, took the coffee, and wrapped both hands around the mug. She brought it close to her face, letting the steam warm her. With eyes closed, she inhaled the aroma.

"Do you always enjoy your coffee without tasting it?"

She sipped before answering. "It's the only way to fully enjoy the flavor." She followed Tristan to one of the tables closest to the windows and couldn't help but feel something different about him. Not able to put her finger on it, uneasiness overtook her. She played with the coffee mug, avoiding eye contact.

Feeling his eyes upon her, she pushed back her chair. "I really should be going. I wanted to get some writing done before dinner." She hurried from the room, then upstairs. She entered her room, locked the door, and sank onto the bed.

What's going on? Is my mind playing tricks on me?

Laptop open, Jayla tried writing. While pondering her plot, her mind wandered. She got up and paced the room, trying to shake the memories that plagued her. She had never faced the event that changed her life.

The memory from three years ago was as clear as glass. She could even see the room in her mind's eye, the walls painted yellow. It wasn't even a *peaceful* yellow. She had looked around the room and wondered what color would bring her happiness. Not one came to mind. The longer she looked, the more failures weighed down on her. She had sat there with a full glass of water and swallowed one pill after another. Just kept taking one more until she emptied the bottle. They made her woozy. The walls faded in and out, as she tried to focus.

The door opening sounded a million miles away. The calling of her name muffled. She remembered no more until she woke up in the hospital. *Another failure* had been her first thought.

Jenna had been sitting there—eyes red from crying—and had never said a word about it. When Jayla was released from the hospital, Jenna hovered around her more than ever. That pivotal moment drove Jayla to move out of her parents' house that she had been sharing with her sister. She needed some distance, but she never got any. Jenna continued to hover.

Overwhelmed with loneliness, Jayla had reached out to her old friend, Ryan. He moved in with her as a roommate, and she'd cried on his shoulder many nights. She had no idea he would think it meant anything more than old friends.

I was wrong…

Jayla moved to the window. Forehead against the cool pane, she forced her thoughts onto the present. She would not go back to those memories anymore. It was better to put them aside and keep them in the past.

She closed her eyes, easing the heat from the hidden pain of her past. Wetness on her cheeks brought her back. Her tears flowed, unchecked. The emptiness continued, and she couldn't fight it anymore. She yearned for that night—so long ago—to have ended differently. If only once she could have succeeded at something—even something so final. Even now, dark thoughts crossed her mind. Loneliness haunted her. It disappeared whenever Tristan was around. Not the *shy* Tristan, but the one that dared to hold her. He ignited a spark she thought she would never feel.

seven

Trenton slid open the door hidden deep in the closet of the back bedroom in the west wing. It revealed a secret passage. He stepped in, hesitating only a second. Revenge needed to be put into place.

He knew all the passages, even without a light. There would be a fork soon. One passage branched to the right and led to the room where Jayla was staying. The other went to Tristan's room. Straight past both branches, he would descend a flight of stairs leading to the living room.

Each room held a tapestry on the wall that covered the passage doors. As kids, they had played in those walls, hiding from their parents, seeing things they weren't meant to see. Trenton smiled at the memory of the first time he brought Tristan with him. Trent had found the passages weeks before and explored them himself. He told Tristan he had a secret. Tristan never was very adventurous, but he followed Trenton anyway. Trenton ran ahead in the dark and coaxed his brother to follow.

He could hear Tristan yelling for him to stop. The fear in his voice enticed Trent to keep just ahead. Finally, he gave in and completely halted. Once Tristan reached him, Trenton called him a baby. But after a few jaunts through the passageways, Tristan was running through them, right along with him.

Trenton came to the branched-off passages and paused. Did he want to see Jayla? He shook his head and started for the opposite tunnel. The plan needed to be put in motion, and he had to know his options. He stopped only when he reached the door in Tristan's room.

He opened the door. The tapestry covered it, and he couldn't be seen. He ran his hand over the back of the heavy cloth to find the one spot that had two small slices in it. He slowly eased one of them apart and scowled, spotting Tristan in front of the window. He looked sad, almost broken.

Trenton knew that feeling. He'd experienced it for years while he waited for Tristan to show up. Trenton hardened his heart and narrowed his eyes. This wasn't the Tristan he wanted to see. He had imagined him enjoying the house, planning for the future as the sole heir of the property.

Trenton's anger was fueled by his fantasies. He failed to acknowledge his brother's turmoil. Trent stepped back into the shadows of the passage and slid the door shut. He took a deep breath and slowly let it out. He needed to rethink how to approach this. How could he get Tristan away from the house so *he* could take over? The identity would not be a problem. They were identical—or used to be. There was only one defining characteristic to distinguish them. No one would ever know.

With his mind whirling, he started back to the west wing. He would need more information. The best place to find it was at the carriage house.

He paused at the next branch again, slipped into the other side, and crept through the passage. At the door behind the tapestry in Jayla's room, he hesitated. Did he really want to spy on her?

His heart thumped harder as he opened the door, having made his decision. Like he'd done with the other tapestry, he ran his hand over the back of the cloth to find the spots he could see through. Jayla was on the bed curled into a ball, crying. Her agony sliced through his heart. He longed to approach her and hold her. The feel of his arms around her earlier had made his mind clear of the real reason he was there.

With a soft sigh, he shut the door and quickly moved back to where he needed to be. In order to get back at Tristan he would need to avoid Jayla. However, at the same time, he needed to keep her away from Tristan. He couldn't afford to have her be collateral in his plans.

Trenton spent the rest of the evening mapping out the house and making detailed notes of Tristan's day. He was predictable, and Trenton had already learned most of his routine by heart. By the time he was finished, the sun was just coming up.

Jayla groaned as the sun shined directly in her eyes. The light was still on in the room and her laptop on the bed beside her. She had fallen asleep, crying. Life just never seemed to change.

Feet on the floor, she held her head in her hands. Her eyes felt like sand was overflowing in them. With each blink, the gritty feeling grated harder, deeper. She softly cursed and started for the bathroom. If lucky, a hot shower would do the trick and wash away the wasted night of tears.

She vowed to call Jenna later that day. First things first, shower, and then a hot cup of coffee to refresh her mind so she could get some writing done. She would not forsake her goal, not now that she finally had the courage to reach for it.

While in the shower, Jayla let her thoughts wander to her writing. The hot water coursed over her as she envisioned different scenes. In a flurry, she finished, her focus on getting her thoughts to the keyboard. She threw on jeans and a tank top, reached for the laptop and a notebook, and headed for the dining room.

MIRRORED DECEPTION

There was only one other couple there. Jayla stopped at their table to make small talk before heading to the little table in the corner. She set down her things and went to grab a mug of coffee. Once settled in the chair, she closed her eyes and inhaled the coffee's aroma before taking a sip. She smiled as she remembered Tristan's fascination with her coffee ritual.

She set the mug aside, flipped open the laptop, and tapped her fingers on the table while she waited for it to boot up.

eight

Trenton surveyed the room. It was the last room in the carriage house, and he'd still found no clues about what had happened to his mother.

He wandered around, picking up a strewn book here and there. Conflicted emotions flowed through him: anger at Tristan for obviously hiding something, anger at the way his childhood ended up, and yet loneliness at missing his twin. They hardened his heart, making him cold.

He sank into a covered chair, dust billowing from it. How badly did he want to hurt Tristan? Would it be worth it? He wanted answers, but the pull of missing Trent was so overwhelming. He leaned forward and cupped his face and let the hurt slice through him. How long had he fought this feeling, the pain of losing his brother?

He had taken a year to confront his father's killer, feeling much older than the mere ten years of age in the presence of the old man. Trenton never imagined the danger he had put himself in. He had trusted justice to be served. Instead, he'd lost his childhood and best friend. Never saw their mother again.

The shadows deepened. He was startled with the sound of scraping at the glass. Jumping up, he ran to look. He narrowed his eyes, realizing that a branch against a window had set his nerves on edge. Would he ever stop looking over his shoulder? He ran his hand through his hair and down the back of his neck.

As he finished straightening the mess in the carriage house, Trenton's mind whirled with the possibilities of telling Tristan he was there. With a growl, he let himself out the door and started down the path to The Cliffhouse. Tristan wouldn't care—he had already proved that by letting so many years go by. Not even bothering to look for him when their mother died.

Trenton stopped just inside the wooded area. Jayla was on the veranda, leaning over the railing. He held his breath and watched in fascination at the hair hanging in her face as she looked at the flowers below the railing. She stood and flipped her hair over her shoulder. His fingers itched to run through the silkiness of it.

He slid further into the darkness when she began looking in his direction. She started down the steps.

MIRRORED DECEPTION

Could she see him? He knew she couldn't, but there was a connection between them. He sensed her presence and wondered if she felt the same thing.

Tristan came out of the house. "Jayla. I've been looking for you. Was thinking of walking along the cliff for a bit. Are you up for joining me?"

"I'd love to." Jayla took one last look at the wooded area and turned toward Tristan, then they disappeared around the house.

Trenton balled his hands into fists at his side. Leave it to his brother to take one more thing from him. He moved along the trees, eyes searching to be sure they were gone before he quickly moved toward the west wing to keep an eye out from the upstairs bedroom. The search of the house would have to wait until everyone was in bed. Whatever he was looking for—proof that Tristan knew he had been alive—he would find in the office or Tristan's room. He was certain of it.

He bounded up the stairs two at a time. The urgency to keep Jayla in sight stirred him. The thought of a walk on the cliff brought bad memories. His dad—his death. Was Jayla in danger? He didn't think so.

He peered out the window. They were nowhere to be seen. With a curse, he turned to the room.

An old bureau to the side caught his eye. The room was dusty from the lack of use. He had chosen to stay in the other bedroom down the hall. He contemplated searching the west wing as he walked slowly toward the bureau. It was, after all, where *he* had stayed all those years.

With a finger, he traced the intricate detail in the dust. He suppressed a sigh as he pulled out the top drawer. *Empty*. He shoved it in with a bang. He reached for the second drawer. *Empty*. He pushed this one in slower and stared at the third and final drawer. It would probably be empty also.

Trenton jumped at a clap of thunder. He jerked around and was at the window in an instant. A storm had quickly crept up. He scanned the walkway along the cliff. Still no signs of Tristan and Jayla. He hoped they were already inside.

Lightning flashed over the water. He missed that sight through the years. The brightness reflecting off the ocean was so magical. His dad had painted it once, but he couldn't remember what had happened to the painting. His mother had hated the storms and she had probably disposed of the painting. He needed more information on what happened to his mother; an understanding of why she never searched for him.

Only one way to find out. He returned to the dresser and yanked out the third drawer. A bundle of letters lay right on top. He stared at them, and then slowly dropped to his knees, recognizing his mom's handwriting on the top envelope. He'd found the connection to her he'd been looking for—something familiar from all those years he missed.

He took the first one, sat on the floor, and leaned against the bed. He ran his fingers over the handwriting, then closed his eyes. He remembered her sitting and writing letters. She had hated being at

The Cliffhouse, so she wrote daily to friends who weren't close by.

The envelope was addressed to Sam, the gardener. Scowling, Trenton took the letter from it. The paper had yellowed with age, and the musty smell assaulted his senses. His stomach clenched with anticipation as he opened that first letter. No turning back now. The letter was dated the year before his father died. As he read through the love endearments proclaimed to Sam from his mother, anticipation turned to nausea. All those years, she had been with Sam, behind his father's back. Did she know about Sam taking him? Or even the truth about her husband's death?

He put the letter back with the others, unable to bring himself to read the rest. Hatred coursed through his blood. His heart tightened as he hardened himself to the loss of his mother. If she knew about him, then Tristan would have, too. Irrational logic fed Trenton's anger. He kicked the drawer as he stood and clenched his hands into tight fists.

He would search the house as soon as it was quiet and locked up for the night.

nine

Just after midnight, Trenton crept down the passageway leading to the living room. Cautiously, he peeked out before slipping from behind the tapestry. He glanced around, letting his eyes adjust to the dark.

Where to look? His eyes swept over the living room. Nothing obvious stood out. He wanted to finish quickly and get out of there. He didn't want to take a chance of any of the guests waking up.

He headed toward the check-in desk in the foyer, staying alert to every sound and became satisfied there was nothing more than usual settlings of a house. He stood behind the desk and ran his hands over the finish, fingers sweeping slightly over the phone. He let himself enjoy the freedom of being there, wishing it was his.

With family thoughts in his mind, he started searching…for something that told where his mother had been, why she died, and more importantly why no one came looking for him.

He found nothing other than business records as he flipped through files.

He stood against the wall. Where else could anything be? No doubt things were in Tristan's room, but he would not be able to search that tonight. From the guest records, all rooms were full. He turned back to the living room. As he slipped behind the tapestry, footsteps entered the living room.

Through the slits in the cloth, he saw Jayla making her way to the kitchen. Her thin tank top hugged her body, and her shorts emphasized her long, sleek legs. Without a thought, he slipped back into the living room and followed.

"Jayla, what are you doing up?" He stood in the doorway as she quickly turned from the refrigerator.

"I didn't think anyone else was awake. I'll pay for what I took." She played with the towel on the countertop in front of her.

"No need. Take what you want." Trenton gestured as he strolled toward her, taking her in from head to toe.

"Did you want something?" Her voice was soft.

"Yeah, um…no." He couldn't take his eyes off her soft lips. He wanted to reach out, pull her close, and feel her against him. "I should go."

He spun around and left. With a glance over his shoulder, he slipped into the passageway. Slowly, he moved back to the west wing and ran his fingers through his hair. How could he have gotten so careless? If he had acted on his impulse, it would have resulted in questions with Tristan in the morning.

Jayla stared after the abrupt departure. What had happened?

She poured herself a glass of orange juice and pondered whether or not it was a good decision to stay there any longer. She couldn't afford to get involved with someone who was obviously conflicted in feelings and so confusing to be around. It didn't take her long to drain the glass. She then washed it and put it away.

She started for the bedroom but was drawn to the bay window in the dining room. So pretty—the moonlight playing on the ocean. A sense of calm flooded her, and she made her decision. She couldn't leave right now. That peacefulness was mandatory.

The place had an internal pull, keeping her there. Beyond the fact that Tristan was very attractive and her preoccupation of trying to figure out how he felt about her, The Cliffhouse had a magnetic quality. Without a doubt, her soul could heal there.

Ten

The waves crashed against the rocks, matching the anger burning inside Trenton. He stood just inside the dense area of the woods. His heart pounded with every crash of the surf. Lights flashed across the yard as Tristan's SUV pulled out. It was now or never—time to search Tristan's room.

With one last look at the ocean, Trenton headed for the house. He needed to slip in and upstairs without anyone noticing. He entered through the back door into the kitchen. It was empty, but someone was clearing the dining room. He quickly moved on quiet feet and made his way to the side stairway. After a glance over his shoulder, he ascended the stairs.

At the top, he paused. Jayla's room was to the left of the hallway and Tristan's down the hall to the right of the stairwell. He felt a tug toward Jayla's room, but had no time to waste, not knowing how long Tristan would be gone. He hugged the wall and moved down the hall. Assured no one was in the vicinity, he slipped into the room, shutting the door silently.

Very neat. Clothes in the closet were in orderly rows, shoes lined on the floor. With a snort of disgust, he turned toward the bureau. Tristan had always kept his treasures in his top drawer.

Trenton froze with his hand poised to pull the drawer out. He gave it a tug, and it slid open. A wooden box lay on top. He carefully moved it out. Tristan's treasure box—the one Trenton had given him as a kid. Trenton had spent hours making it for his twin. He ran his hand over the smooth grain. His dad had helped him glue the sides together. He had worked so hard sanding. He smiled, remembering how his dad had let him stain the wood and never said a word about the mess that resulted. He had chosen a walnut color, not too dark, that had brought out the natural grain in the wood.

Tristan had been thrilled to receive it for his birthday. He promised to always hold a piece of Trenton in it. Trenton, now staring down at it, feared opening the lid to see if Tristan had kept his promise. He tentatively slid the cover open. Right on top lay the same picture of him and Tristan that he carried with him. With a soft release of breath, Trenton picked it up. He closed his eyes, remembering the day the picture was taken. They were not quite nine. They had spent the day flying kites with their father, both boys' cheeks reddened by the wind, smiles radiating their happiness.

He set the picture aside, turned back to the box, and found an obituary for his mom. Even through tears, he managed to read it. She had died after a lengthy sickness. He questioned what was wrong with her and had no idea where she died. The obituary simply said, *died after a long stay in the hospital.* He imagined the worst thing he could possibly think of – *cancer.*

He allowed his mind to play into the imagery of her lying there alone, dying, cancer ravaging her body. He cleared his mind with a hard head shake and stared down at the obituary clutched between two of his fingers. He placed it beside him on top of the picture and turned back to the box. A letter folded numerous times was next. He picked it up and slowly started unfolding it.

The writing had faded and the folds had become fragile from frequently being folded and unfolded. He moved closer to the window for the light to hit the paper. The handwriting was unfamiliar, yet it spoke of *his* death. Trenton stared out the window. Focused on nothing, he felt wetness against his cheek. He wiped his hand across his face, startled at the tears that flowed from him. Who would write to Tristan and tell him that his brother was dead? Was it possible that all those years Tristan believed he was dead and that's why he hadn't come for him?

He crumpled the paper and threw it at the bureau. Trenton swore under his breath as the paper deflected off the top and fell down behind. He needed to keep control at all times. Tristan couldn't know someone had been in his room.

Trenton gathered everything to put it all back into the box. He hesitated about getting the letter. Shrugging, he threw the box in the top drawer and slid it shut. He didn't believe any of it. He concluded that Tristan must somehow know that his twin was back and planted the phony letter.

He glanced around the room one more time. Voices in the hallway put him in motion. He slid behind the tapestry and into the passage. He listened, as there was a knock at the door. Not lingering, he hurried toward the west wing.

It was time to take back what was rightfully his, what he had come back for.

eleven

Trenton stood in the wooded glen and watched the house. There wasn't much activity, except his brother tending to the front flowerbeds. Even after so many years, the similarity between them was amazing. They had the same build and style of hair. How could two people who were separated for so long still be so identical?

Hatred burned in his heart. Tristan had the easy life. Living it up, going to school, probably dating all the pretty girls, and now running the family business. Trenton's life had not mirrored his brother's. His education was what he had gained from the internet. He read everything he could get his hands on and longed for his GED. The ache from the realization of how much was ripped from his life at such a tender age hardened his heart daily to the life around him.

In recent years, Trenton had done well for himself. He worked off and on as a handyman, moving from town to town and saving his money. He had no place to bank it, as his identity still needed to be kept secret—at least until he knew where things stood with his family. He wished there had been the opportunity to talk to his mother and find out just what she was aware of regarding his father's death.

His brother, who had left him to rot all those years, had a bright future. His mother, who reiterated her seemingly lack of love for Trenton by not rescuing him, fighting for him. His father—who died a horrible death at the hands of Sam. And Sam…a man he had always looked up to as a child, until the day he witnessed the tragic event.

Trenton clenched his hands into fists as he willed his anger to calm. He wanted nothing more than to approach Tristan and blast him for his lack of caring. They were twins. Didn't that mean anything? Trenton had thought it did, but that thought died a little with every year that passed without contact from his brother.

He had continued to search the papers. There had been no word of his abduction. Why would they hide that?

He turned on his heel and strode through the woods with purpose in his step. He would not let Tristan get away with taking the family business. Trenton had a right to it, and he would claim it.

MIRRORED DECEPTION

He slowed as he entered the clearing to the cottage. His hands had relaxed, and he flexed them to release the tension from his shoulders.

Where to begin?

He pulled the tarp from his motorcycle, grabbed the helmet, and straddled the bike. He started the motor and turned toward the center of town. It would be the best place to start nosing around.

It was a short drive, and he relaxed as he became one with the bike. He parked in front of the local diner, shut off the bike, and took off his helmet. The town was certainly slow for this time of year. Suddenly, he remembered trips into town with his dad, and he smiled as he thought of all the candy his dad bought him while they were out buying supplies for the bed-and-breakfast. The candy was their secret as his mother would have had a fit.

Cool air assaulted him as he stepped inside the diner and made his way to the back booth and slid in. Most tables were empty. A few were filled with people he didn't recognize. His eyes rested on the waitress making a fresh pot of coffee. She looked vaguely familiar, but he couldn't place her. He was on dangerous ground and had to tread lightly not to give away his real identity. With any luck, most people would take him for Tristan, and he could steer the conversation to The Cliffhouse and its summer business.

The waitress set a cup of steaming coffee in front of Trenton and smiled. "Hiding in the back today? I assume you want the usual, Trist."

"Absolutely."

"Be right back."

He watched her walk away and smirked at the slight sway of her hips. Was she the type Tristan went for? She definitely wasn't *his* type. Too forward.

He sipped his coffee while watching the other customers. A young couple, obviously tourists, giggled and talked over their breakfast, phones in hands taking pictures of their breakfast. Pictures that would probably be posted on social media within minutes.

He leaned back as the waitress returned to his table. She slid a plate of bacon, eggs, and home fries in front of him.

"Thanks."

He glanced at her as she slid into the booth. "Haven't seen you for a while, Tristan. Where have you been hiding?" She batted her eyes at him.

"Busy with the bed-and-breakfast. You know how it is. Why don't you fill me in on what's been happening here in town?" He ate, giving her the opportunity to talk.

"Oh, the usual. You know I don't gossip. But Momma did say she hadn't seen you in a while and wanted you to stop by."

Trenton finished his coffee and pushed the plate aside. "I'll try and do that soon. Got a lot going on right now with the busy season coming up."

"I know, but she misses seeing you. Me, too."

He smiled lazily at the pout she put on her lips. He could easily play with the situation to torment Tristan, but he just couldn't bring himself to do that. He couldn't toy with the girl's emotions, even if Tristan was serious about her. It just wasn't an area he would lower himself to. He wanted to hurt Tristan, not innocent bystanders.

"I'll see you later." He threw down money on the table and stood.

"Tristan?" She stood up and he could feel her eyes on his back as he headed for the door. He raised his hand in a wave and slipped out the door. Although the breakfast had been good comfort food, the waitress' obvious affection for his brother added a layer of guilt that he didn't want to deal with.

He walked down the sidewalk and stopped in front of the general store. He wondered if ole man Jim still ran the place. Back then, he had seemed ancient to Trenton, but in reality, the man couldn't have been older than mid-sixties. He would be old now, but possibly still around.

He shrugged as he started back for his motorcycle. Something he just wasn't ready to face yet. Someday, he would come into town and everyone would know him for himself, *Trenton*, without the necessity of pretending to be Tristan.

He took the secondary road back to the bed-and-breakfast and turned toward the ocean. He enjoyed the cool air whipping at him as he cruised along the oceanside drive. The road was empty, and he was able to just enjoy the beauty he had missed for so many years.

As usual, his mind drifted to Tristan. How close would they be now if they hadn't grown up away from one another? Would they be more alike or would Trenton still have a harder side to him? Adventure had been in his blood as a child. He had no urge to settle down. He didn't need a family. He had a family once, and that didn't get him far. His heart hard, Trenton scowled as he picked up his speed, anxious to return to his haven in the west wing.

He carefully covered the motorcycle after the muffler cooled, then sat on the porch steps of the cottage, contemplating his next move. Tristan obviously wasn't one to hang out in town. He needed to find out exactly how well the bed-and-breakfast was doing.

The pounding in his head started again. Trenton closed his eyes and rubbed his fingers in a circular motion on his temples. Headaches had plagued him for years. They started after he first began fighting his abductor. Being whipped and beaten was the reward for his courage. He splayed his fingers across his forehead and just held his head. Trenton had yet to have his headaches fully checked, but with the frequency of late, it would eventually have to be done. One trip to the ER on a particularly bad night was all he had mustered up to do.

With a groan, he pushed himself to a standing position. The darkness of the west wing should help. Besides, his medication was there. A prescription he was careful about using, because he had no way to get more. He moved cautiously through the woods and made his way to The Cliffhouse. Standing in the shadows, he watched guests arriving. He would have to wait until dark to get to the house.

He startled alert when Jayla came into view. She scanned the wooded area, and he shrank back against a tree. Since she couldn't see him in the shadows, he took the chance to observe her.

Her hair hung freely around her shoulders. She was without the laptop that she usually carted around everywhere. His gaze traveled down her long, brown legs that seemed to go on forever from the hem of her shorts to her sandaled feet. The flexing muscles in her legs as she strolled down the stairs had him swallowing hard. The simple movement of pushing the hair out of her face brought an ache that he had never felt before. Oh, he had been with women, but never had he felt a connection with anyone as he did Jayla.

The sound of a car coming up the driveway made him step backward even farther as the car parked and Tristan stepped out. Trent scowled as his brother approached Jayla. He couldn't hear their exchange of words, but the smile that spread across her face brought a burn to Trenton's insides. He had never truly experienced jealousy before, and the envy he felt for his brother at that moment took him by surprise.

He sharply turned and headed back to the cottage. The throbbing in his head intensified, and he hoped lying down might bring some relief from the pain. It would be hours before nightfall when he could get back to the west wing.

Twelve

Trenton set down the bag and surveyed the kitchen. He had to admit that Tristan had hired the best of the best for kitchen help. Not a speck of dirt anywhere. Food was excellent.

His conscience had kicked in after meeting Jayla in the kitchen the other night. He didn't want to hurt anyone, especially her, but needed to start extracting revenge on his brother. The house was quiet and the timing perfect for putting the plan in motion.

He scanned the ceiling and found the appropriate smoke/fire detectors in place. There was also a sprinkler system. The damage from the sprinklers would be enough for a start.

He opened the refrigerator and helped himself to the left-over chicken parmesan he had smelled as they served dinner. Providing dinner to the guests was something new Tristan had started. Although The Cliffhouse was still considered a bed-and-breakfast, obviously Tristan wanted to offer the guests more when he included other meals.

Trenton reheated the food and sat at the bar, enjoying the meal. Upon finishing, he washed his dishes, dried them, and put them away exactly as he found them. So far, no one knew he ate nightly. The food was so good, he considered keeping the kitchen staff on when he took over ownership of The Cliffhouse.

He pulled out two ping-pong balls from the bag. Smirking, he pictured Tristan's face when he realized his kitchen would have to be shut down for a few days. He would feel obligated to cater breakfast and possibly dinner for his guests, cutting into his profits.

Trenton had seen the balance sheets. The Cliffhouse made a pretty penny, even during the offseason. The summer season *more* than paid for the rest of the year.

He made sure everything was in order, placed the smoke bomb in the sink, and lit it. He reached up and knocked out the sprinkler pin to start the sprinklers, then raced to the hidden doorway in the living room and started to the west wing. Within seconds, the smoke detectors went off, and Trenton stopped in his tracks.

The urge to turn and go back to watch struck him. He shook his head, knowing full well that the only reason he wanted to go back was to make sure Jayla wasn't hurt. With a pang of conscience, Trenton continued walking.

Tristan awoke to the beeping of smoke detectors. *What the . . .?*

He jumped from the bed, reached for his jeans, and slid into them. He rushed to the door and flung it open. Chaos greeted him in the hallway as guests came pouring out of their rooms asking questions.

"I'm not sure what is going on yet," he said as calmly as possible, "but the best thing would be for you to wait outside on the veranda for now." Tristan gestured in that direction and raced for the stairs. He hadn't seen Jayla in the hallway.

"Tristan!" He had just reached the foyer when Jayla screamed his name.

"Jayla, what happened?"

She hastened toward him. "I called nine-one-one."

"Good. What happened?"

"I was coming downstairs for a drink when the alarm went off. I saw smoke coming from the kitchen."

Tristan immediately headed in that direction.

Jayla grabbed his arm and stopped him. "Don't go in there. You don't know how bad the fire is. Wait for the fire department."

"I can't. I need to minimize the damage, if possible." He hurried to the kitchen door and pushed it open. Smoke poured out, blinding him, so he threw a hand over his eyes and stayed in the doorway. Water from the sprinklers rained down. His eyes burned from the smoke, yet he managed to peer through the haze and saw no fire. There was no heat.

"Tristan, they're here!" Jayla called from the foyer.

Firefighters stormed into the kitchen.

"Sir, move back." The chief and two others edged past Tristan. "We need to shut off the sprinkler system, sir. No fire, looks like just smoke in here."

"The main valve is right off the kitchen where the water heater is."

The chief poked around the kitchen, then pointed at the sink. "Looks like a smoke bomb was set off here."

Tristan ran his fingers through his hair. *Smoke bomb? Who would do this to him?*

"Sir?" Tristan looked up to see the fire chief watching him. "I'm Chief Robinson. I'll need to talk with you and your guests."

"What's the damage?" Tristan asked. "It was so smoky, I couldn't tell how bad it is."

"Yes, lots of smoke *and* water. No fire at all. Either the sprinklers malfunctioned or they were set off manually." He gestured to the living room. "Is there a place we can talk?"

"Sure. In there." Tristan moved toward the living room. He paced in front of the tapestry hanging on the wall. "How did this happen?"

"That's what we'd like to know. Are you aware of anyone who'd want to damage the bed-and-breakfast?"

"No. I can't imagine. All the guests seem happy, no one is disgruntled." Tristan stared at the chief. "You don't think *I'm* responsible for this, do you?"

"I have no suspects at this point, but I will need to talk to your guests. I'd like to start with the young lady who called it in."

"Jayla Ralston." Tristan pointed to the foyer where she waited. Her hair was down from her ponytail. Even disheveled she was beautiful. "She arrived a couple of weeks ago and had planned to stay through the summer."

"If you don't mind, I need to talk with her alone, Mr. Montgomery."

"I understand." Tristan moved toward the door. "Jayla, the chief has some questions for you."

Her eyes were wider than ever. If only Tristan could reach out and pull her to him.

Jayla walked slowly toward the living room. Chief Robinson gestured to the other side of the room, and she followed him.

Tristan stepped outside where the rest of the guests were milling on the veranda. "The fire chief is going to have some questions for all of you."

A barrage of questions ensued, so Tristan put his hand up to stop them. "I have no answers right now. Please answer any questions asked of you, and I will update you as soon as I know more."

He moved off the veranda and stood in the driveway facing the woods. *What a nightmare...* He looked back at the house. Lights were on. The damage had been confined to the kitchen. Tristan's mind reeled.

Who could have done this to him? One of his guests, or someone else? He didn't have enemies…that he knew of. Damaged kitchen. Damn, he needed to find a caterer for tomorrow morning, and it was late. He closed his eyes and inhaled deeply. This could not be happening.

The west wing of the house was dark as usual. He once again contemplated renovating that part of the house to have more rooms. A part of him held on to the memories and needed it to stay the same. He hadn't set foot in that wing since his mother died. He'd spent hours just sitting in the living room after he had admitted his mother to the psych ward. The pain of missing Trenton had been even stronger then. The weight of running the bed-and-breakfast was overwhelming. The longing for his twin brother to be there running it with him had been strong. He still missed their childhood days. Why were the memories so much stronger as of late?

He started back for the house, shaking off the blues. He needed to assess the damage and find a caterer.

Thirteen

Trenton lay on the bed, smirking. The fire department had been present for hours and questioned everyone. Tristan was panicking, trying to find a caterer. Unfortunately, the loyal kitchen staff offered to make pastries and a cold breakfast to be served in the morning.

He had overheard the fire chief stating a smoke bomb had been set, but they had no leads for the moment. Trenton didn't believe they had ruled out Tristan as of yet. He swung his legs over the edge of the bed and dropped his head into his hands. He hated that Jayla had been put through the questioning.

The room suddenly felt stifling. He moved to the window and looked out at the ocean. The reflection from the moon's light danced off the water like crystals. He sighed as the anguish engulfed him, and he closed his eyes. This was supposed to be a happy place for him. Why was he feeling so wrong about everything?

Fresh air would do him wonders right now. He rushed downstairs and ran out the back door. Slipping out into the shadows, he moved quickly to the line of trees at the edge of the woods. He crept to the cliff, overlooking the ocean, and stayed in the shadows. Trenton crouched and sat on the edge of the cliff. He could never get enough of the thunderous sound from the water crashing against the rocks below. It brought him peace and calmness.

He flashed back to that night, as a child, watching his father go over the cliff. He could only imagine the pain his father had felt hitting the jagged rocks below. His chest tightened. With each breath he took, it felt like a vice grip had hold of him. His breath came in short spurts now, quicker as the panic started to rise up in him. He focused in on taking a deep breath, shutting out the memory of his dad, until his breathing evened out and the tightness in his chest lessened.

Trenton shook off the hollow feeling and the nightmare left behind and allowed his thoughts to move to Jayla.

Out of the corner of his eye, he saw the light in her room. She appeared to be staring out the window. Her hair was down, flowing over her shoulders. With the light behind her, he could see the tank top she wore was form-fitting, and he felt a longing to touch her.

He cautiously stood from the cliff's edge and inched back into the shadows. Being careful to stay hidden, he moved farther into the woods. The carriage house would be the best place to stay for now. He needed space between him and Jayla, and to figure out how to get her alone, away from Tristan. He wanted to spend more time with her. The few interactions they'd had were impersonal, due to the fact that he had to pretend to be someone else. He wanted to pull her against him and…

With a growl, he hurried his pace to a slow jog. His mind had to remain clear.

A shiver ran through Jayla. Was someone watching through those deep, dark shadows?

Tristan had been a mess after the fire department left, and she longed to get far away from him. He was not the man who brought a fiery ache to her stomach. The man she was attracted to only revealed himself in glimpses.

Sighing, she picked up her laptop and allowed herself to slip into another world as she wrote. The characters and plot took her away from reality and into a world where she could control the outcome. When she finished the chapter, she realized over two hours had gone by, and it was early morning.

Not tired, she decided to take a walk along the

cliff and clear her mind. There were decisions to be made. She slid a sweatshirt over her tank top as she ran down the stairs. Once she stepped out onto the veranda, she pulled her hair back into a ponytail to keep it from whipping around her face in the wind. The fresh salt air brought a wide smile and a deep, cleansing breath. Jayla closed her eyes and allowed the tension to roll off her shoulders.

She glanced toward the woods and decided to skip the cliff walk and follow the path instead. She found herself humming as she went along and stopped every so often to listen to the birds. The woods were full of commotion early in the morning. Squirrels chattered over acorns, and birds called out to one another.

"Jayla."

The soft voice caught her off guard and she quickly swung to her left. Seeing Tristan, she warily looked around.

"Did you sleep well?" he asked.

"I didn't really sleep. Got caught up in writing, and then I wasn't tired. Decided to do a little sightseeing instead."

His face lit up. "Care for some company? The old family cottage is just through the woods here."

"Sure." Jayla moved slowly toward him and hesitated to grab his hand when he reached out to her, yet took it regardless. The warmth of his touch as he intertwined his fingers with hers sent heat radiating down to her toes. The tingling started, and suddenly, her mind was clear and yet foggy at the same time.

She shivered, and subconsciously moved closer to Tristan. "You are a very confusing man."

He glanced over at her. "What do you mean?"

"I get such mixed signals from you. One moment warm and friendly, and the next, almost standoffish."

He shrugged. "I didn't realize I was doing that. I try to act professional around all the guests, but away from the house..." His voiced teasingly trailed off.

Jayla smiled and relaxed. She was surprised to feel relief and knew it meant she really liked the guy.

The cottage came into sight. It was aged with weather, but in good shape. The slate shingles were intact, or at least had been repaired as needed. "What a beautiful place. Did you grow up here?"

He squeezed her hand. "I grew up in the B&B, but this was my dad's painting studio. I spent hours here with him. He taught me woodworking."

Jayla watched his face as the memories softened the lines and radiated love. He glanced at her, and just as quickly, his confusing mask fell back into place. Why was he always so conflicted?

"Sounds like good memories for you." She slipped her hand out of his and walked toward the house. "You must have been very close to your dad."

"I was." His voice trembled. "He died when I was nine."

"I'm so sorry. I know what it's like to lose your parents. Mine were killed in a car accident a few years back." Jayla faced the house. "The pain never seems to go away, just lessens from day to day."

She moved slowly up the stairs to the porch.

It was empty, but she could envision rockers with cushions, Tristan and his dad sitting there drinking lemonade. She smiled and turned toward him. "Why don't you stay here more?"

"I do some. It's hard with the B&B. Duty calls for me to be there." He leaned against the railing. "Not as if my brother is around to help out."

Jayla tilted her head, intently watching his face. There was hurt in his eyes and voice as he spoke.

"Haven't seen him in years," he went on. "Obviously, he doesn't care about being in the family business."

Puzzled by his answer, Jayla moved toward the stairs. "I'm going to head back. Suddenly a night without sleep is hitting me."

"Jayla?" Trenton placed his hand on her arm to stop her from leaving, then slowly pulled her around to face him.

Her eyes were full of anticipation as he lowered his head and brushed his lips gently across hers. Her sigh sent a shiver through him as he nibbled her bottom lip and along her jawline. Desire engulfed him as her fingers slid into his hair. He captured her lips again, his kiss gentle, but demanding. Feeling her respond, he slowing pulled away.

"Maybe you should go." He took a step back. His breath felt ragged, and he longed for nothing more than to take her inside the cottage and find a soft bed.

Her tongue ran over her lips. "I'll see you later." Her voice cracked and her legs seemed to shake as she started for the path through the woods.

How did that happen and why was she running away? Was she actually *running,* or had he pushed her away? It was all a blur.

He watched her until she disappeared from view. He leaned on the railing and cursed to himself. If she had kissed Tristan already, he may have just blown his cover. Still, he couldn't resist her softness, the gentleness she showed toward him. The kiss had been worth the risk.

fourteen

Tristan started down the stairs. He had tossed and turned for a couple of hours after the firefighters finally left. He couldn't believe someone would deliberately sabotage his bed-and-breakfast. Yet, suddenly, events that had taken place over the past few weeks came back to him. He had had a few deliveries not show up with any rhyme or reason, throwing off the kitchen and menu. He'd simply chalked it up to a miscommunication with the vendors.

Then there were the times the electricity went out at the most inopportune moments. Several guests had checked out early as a result. The repairmen had found nothing wrong with the wiring, but a breaker had shut off. For it to happen more than once...were those events all just coincidences, or was someone behind them?

He stopped at the check-in desk and went through the guest list. The fire department had asked that everyone stay at least another week. Thankfully no one had been slated to check out before then, so there wouldn't be any more loss in profits. Unless, of course, more mishaps occurred.

He set the papers aside and perched on the stool. His thoughts drifted to Jayla. She had seemed so frightened when the fire chief asked to speak to her. The urge to hold her close was strong, but he had curbed it, yet he had gone to see her early that morning. There had been no answer when he knocked on her door. Sighing, he stood. It was time to survey the damage in the daylight.

He had already made a call to a cleaning company and expected them to arrive momentarily. He pushed open the kitchen door and took in the smoke stains on the walls, heaviest over the sink. Water marks on the floor and bottom cupboards were evident. He had called the insurance company and expected the adjuster to arrive about the same time as the cleaning company. It was going to be a long day.

The throbbing in his temples grew. He headed to the dining room for some strong coffee. He had just taken his first sip when the insurance adjuster arrived. Mark Sullivan and he had grown up together.

"Mark, how about some coffee?" Tristan gestured toward the coffee urn on the sideboard.

"Would love some," Mark said.

Tristan set down his own cup and moved to fill another one. "What are we looking at?" He handed the mug to Mark. "I can't believe this, right in the middle of our busy season."

"Well, we'll look at the damages and get an estimate for the cost of cleaning. The cleaning company should be here today, right?" Mark glanced at his notes. "From what I'm reading in the fire report, looks like the damage was contained to the kitchen, which is good."

"Yeah." Tristan sipped his coffee.

"It should be a pretty clear-cut claim. The only question is, the chief felt it could have been deliberately done by someone. Once that's determined, we can finalize the claim."

"Yeah, that's what he said. I just don't know who would do that to me."

"Let's check out the kitchen. Maybe some answers will come to light." Mark downed the last of his coffee and stood. "Ready?"

"As I'll ever be." Tristan led the way to the kitchen. He stood in the doorway while Mark took measurements and made notes on his notepad. The silence was deafening.

Out of the corner of his eye, Tristan caught a glimpse of Jayla tiptoeing across the foyer and hurrying up the stairs. Why would she be sneaking in this early in the morning?

Finalizing cleaning, signing estimates, and authorizing the clean-up, took the whole morning. By the time Tristan could slip away, his head was pounding. Most of the guests had left for the day, stating they were going to do sightseeing and grab lunch and dinner out. The goal was for the kitchen to be up and running within a couple of days. He placed calls to the local diners, setting up arrangements for him to be billed directly for any of his customers who ate there.

Tristan headed upstairs to shower, and his mind wandered to Jayla and about how he had seen her sneaking in early that morning. He wondered if he had read her wrong. Could she have sabotaged his kitchen? Although he found her company enjoyable, he really knew nothing about her. She was very closed-mouth regarding her family and past. Though, he couldn't imagine any reason she might have to do such a thing.

As he thought about it, he realized he knew nothing about the other guests either, but the simple fact that Jayla was returning to the bed-and-breakfast at that time of day made his suspicions run wild.

After his shower, he felt more relaxed and quickly dressed in a pair of khaki shorts and light blue shirt. He needed to check on the progress of the cleaning crew before heading into town to run errands.

Trenton pulled the tarp off his motorcycle. He needed to get away, at least for the day. The thrill of kissing Jayla boosted his spirits, yet at the same time his conscience kicked in, and he questioned whether or not the smoke bomb had been a smart idea. He didn't truly want to hurt Tristan, he just needed him out of the bed-and-breakfast, out of town, and away from the homestead.

He needed to clear his head, so he straddled the bike and took off with the wind blowing through his hair. After a couple of miles, his muscles relaxed, and he was able to enjoy the scenery of the coastal route.

For years now, riding had been his escape. Some days, he tried to outrun the memories that plagued him. The taste of Jayla on his lips couldn't be outrun, though. Suddenly, revenge didn't seem so sweet. Jayla had proven to put a crimp in his plans, and he was at a loss how to react to that.

He turned onto a dirt road, really no wider than a trail. His thoughts went to his dad. He had been taken from life so young. Had his father known the secret life his mother was leading?

Trenton had paid little attention to the road he knew so well and was surprised to arrive at the cabin his father had loved so much.

Trenton dismounted and stood in the drive with his hands on his hips. It hadn't changed at all in the years since he had last seen it. Tears filled his eyes as he walked up the stairs. He knew exactly where to find the key. He pushed open the door to find layers of dust everywhere, evidence that no one had used the cabin recently.

He spent the next few hours cleaning and making it ready. This was the place Jayla could hear the truth, if he allowed himself the liberty of letting go of the past.

By the time he locked up the cabin and headed toward The Cliffhouse, it was dusk. The sun played off the ocean as it dipped down, the sky a reddish-orange hue. The sunset gave him hope that there could be a brighter future. The only taint on it would be the battle with Tristan.

fifteen

The crew didn't take long to clean the smoke damage. Tristan was pleased with the progress, and the fact that he didn't lose income as a result of the incident. There still were no leads on who was behind it.

Mark had checked in with him several times over the past few days, and that morning's phone call confirmed the settlement of the claim. The insurance company would be closing their file. Tristan's understanding was that if the intruder was ever found, the insurance firm would subrogate against them to recover their costs.

His mood was buoyed by his guests not having to leave to eat. He decided tomorrow's evening meal would be *on the house* as a thank you to his guests for sticking through the disaster with him.

He went to the window and his eye caught Jayla, heading for the rose garden. He moved closer to watch. She was attractive, and he enjoyed her company, but she just didn't ignite chemistry in him. Sighing, he turned back to the desk to finish some paperwork.

In all the years he had been running the bed-and-breakfast, a day didn't go by that he didn't wish his brother was helping him. Trenton had been the strong one. Through the whole insurance ordeal, Tristan missed his brother more than ever.

With the balance sheets finished for the day, he packed up the desk of loose papers and started for the door. Maybe Jayla would want to go for a walk. Her company was always calming. Being a twin herself, maybe she could understand the longing he felt for his brother, even after so many years. He hadn't mentioned much to her regarding Trenton, and now he longed to share his thoughts with someone.

He turned the corner to the arbored-entrance of the rose garden and stopped short. Jayla's head was bent over the closed laptop on her lap. Her hair flowed freely in front of her face. From the shaking of her shoulders, he assumed she was crying. Conflicted whether to go and comfort her or to leave her be, he settled for the latter and backed away from the garden.

He moved onto the cliff walk. What would she be sad about? Had the incident with the damage in the kitchen upset her that much? What was she truly running from?

Trenton stood in the shadows of the forest and watched his brother move away from the rose garden. Trenton's memories of their mom were intense there and he had only visited it a couple of times since hiding at the Cliffhouse. The urge to see Jayla was too strong to turn back now. He figured Tristan wouldn't return for a while, so Trenton decided to allow himself five minutes to talk with her before getting out of sight.

He moved quietly. "Jayla," he called out in a soft voice, so as not to scare her.

She looked up, and the redness of her eyes tore his heart. He wanted to take that pain from her, protect her from whatever haunted her.

"What is it?" He sat next to her and placed his arm around her shoulders, allowing her to move into him, yet not drawing her close.

"It's nothing." Her back stiffened and she wiped her eyes.

"Jayla, talk to me." When she didn't move away, Trenton enfolded her in his embrace, and she softened.

"Really, Tristan, it's nothing."

Reality slapped him in the face when he heard his brother's name. The feel of her hand putting pressure on his arm brought his focus to her. "I meant no harm. I just hate to see you so broken up..." Trenton stood and moved away, then wandered around the closest rose bushes. The yellow roses held his attention as he kept his back to her. How could he get through to her, gain her trust?

His breath caught when she came up behind him and touched him. "I'm sorry," she said. "I'm just so used to shutting everyone out. I just can't open up…"

He stood still, waiting for more, when he felt her retreat. He turned and reached for her. "Jayla, please."

His eyes searched hers, and he saw the vulnerability in them. He kicked himself mentally for playing this game with her, and he backed off. "We can talk later."

He left the garden, moving quickly to the trees with a glance over his shoulder to make sure she wasn't watching. Once in the shadows, he sucked in a deep breath, cursing the man he had become, and yet wanting to be the man Jayla made him feel he could be.

Emptiness filled Jayla as Tristan left the garden. *That* was the man who had her dreaming of more, who reminded her she wanted a family and the love her parents had shared. Why wasn't he consistent in the way he responded to her? Or was she the problem? Maybe she didn't know how to be consistent.

She opened the laptop and allowed herself the luxury of moving into a different world—the world of writing where she could control the outcome—the escape she craved more and more often.

She raised her eyes with a start as shadows danced across her keyboard. The sun had set and the air had chilled. She saved her work and closed the cover, then got up and went to the edge of the cliff walk. Below, the waves played havoc with one another over the rocks. The soft crashing noise released any further tension in her shoulders, and she sighed.

The time was coming for her to call her sister. She didn't want to place any more worry on her. She had found her strength in writing and was ready to deal with the inevitable confrontation with Jenna.

She turned toward the house, and her gaze moved to the west wing. Tristan had said it wasn't used, but she swore a curtain moved. Eyes intense upon the window, she saw nothing but darkness. Her vision had been strained enough with the use of the computer all day. It had to be a draft that moved the curtain.

She shrugged as she started back. There was no longer any fear in her. She was ready to move on in her life and make what she wanted become reality.

sixteen

Jayla sank into the bed as the day's exhaustion overwhelmed her. It had been a long, few days, and she kept replaying that kiss over and over again. She avoided Tristan for the most part, making a quick escape when she came into contact with him. He seemed standoffish, which bothered her. The question of whether he regretted the kiss plagued her, and she found herself worrying if she put him off, either by her response or her coolness afterward. It was a double-edged sword that pricked her with every thought.

The cell phone woke her from a deep sleep. With a groan, she picked it up, expecting it to be Jenna's number, and planning to hit ignore. She'd been calling repeatedly, numerous times a day. However, Jayla didn't recognize the number flashing on the caller ID.

"Hello?"

"Where are you?" Ryan's sharp, deep voice came across the line. "I've been waiting for you in the parking lot at the apartment. You wouldn't be avoiding me, would you?"

"Ryan? Why are you there? I told you there was nothing between us and you needed to move on." Jayla sighed. This was not what she needed at the moment.

"I think we should talk about it. Tell me where you are, and I'll come to you."

"No. Don't call me again and stop sitting outside *my* apartment."

She heard a deep laugh before the line went dead. Dread filled her. Was this what it was like to be stalked? She would have to face him at some point, just not now. She played with the cell phone, contemplating calling Jenna. If she knew Ryan was outside the apartment, she would be furious with her for not calling sooner.

She'd had enough confrontation for one day, so she killed the power to the phone and lay back against the pillows. She rested her arm over her eyes as she fought to squash the panic rising within her. She fell into a restless sleep, tossing and turning with dreams of being stalked.

Trenton watched Jayla through the tapestry. Whoever called her agitated her. His stomach clenched in anger, and he resisted the urge to push into the room and gather her into his arms. The desire to taste her again had him hardly sleeping. He had tried to focus on the revenge, but she'd gotten under his skin. What had happened? Over the last week, the desire to hurt Tristan had lessened and his feelings for Jayla increased. How had he lost control?

He softly closed the door behind the tapestry and crept down the passageway back to the west wing. For the first time in his life, he was conflicted about what to do. The desire to love and *be* loved was strong, but would it overrule his anger and desire for justice?

He sighed as he fell onto the couch in the west wing. His mind spun the idea of wooing Jayla, and he smiled. He had observed Tristan with her and there seemed to be no chemistry between them. Tristan had his hands full with cleaning up smoke damage and running the B&B. Surely, Jayla must be conflicted if she was at all as affected by the kiss as he was, only to be slighted by Tristan now.

An idea took hold. He would woo her away from the B&B and give her the impression that while at The Cliffhouse he had his hands full and had to stay professional. Once he achieved peace with his desire for Jayla, he could concentrate on revenge and take back what was his.

✢ ✢ ✢

Jayla sipped her morning coffee and ran through her mind different scenarios of calling Jenna. None ended up well for her. With a sigh, she stared out at the ocean. The rolling waves mesmerized her and brought her a sense of calm. She had been there for two weeks, and it felt like a lifetime. She could stay forever and forget the rest of the world. If only it was possible.

The call from Ryan had raised an alarm. What if he still had access to her apartment? He had left the key behind, but maybe he had made a copy. She assumed he didn't if he was sitting outside waiting. Maybe she should call the police. She could at least give them a heads-up that he was stalking her. But was it stalking? Or had she asked for the whole mess by unknowingly leading him on—as he had accused her of doing?

The laptop sat open before her, keys untouched, as she played with the coffee mug. Her cell phone lay at her fingertips.

"How's the writing going this morning, Jayla?" Tristan's deep voice broke through her thoughts.

"Um, it's not really."

"This is the first time I've seen you when you haven't been typing away."

Jayla focused in on Tristan, trying to clear her head. "I know. Just too much on my mind, I guess."

"Anything you want to talk about?"

She flipped her laptop shut and stood. "No, thanks. I think I'll go for a walk and clear my head."

MIRRORED DECEPTION

After putting her computer in the room and locking up, Jayla started outdoors. The cliff walk beckoned her, but the wooded path's call was stronger. She longed to be at the cottage to think. Since she wouldn't run into Tristan—having just left him in the dining room—she meandered through the woods, taking in the sounds and smells. Lost in thought, she wandered into the clearing in front of the cottage before she even realized it. She stopped, surprised she'd already gotten there.

The cottage was well maintained. Again, she pictured rockers on the porch, yet this time with kids running around. Her thoughts moved to that special moment. *The kiss*. She'd been unable to get it out of her mind.

She ran her tongue over her lips, eyes closed remembering the feel. Not just physical, but the feelings it had awakened in her that she had long stopped believing someone would evoke in her. She opened her eyes and walked toward the cottage. Why was she there? There was such a draw to the place, a feeling of love forgotten.

She sat on the stairs leading to the porch. How long had the cottage been empty? She mentally filed it away to ask Tristan about it when she went back. Maybe he would rent it to her for the rest of the summer. It was so peaceful and soothing with the crash of the waves in the background, yet even more private than The Cliffhouse. Sighing, she stood and headed back.

At the edge of the clearing, she turned to get one

last glimpse of the cottage. She was dying to go inside and look, but knew she should have permission first.

She pivoted and began walking back toward the B&B, then slowed her steps. Goosebumps appeared on her arms. The feeling of being watched was undeniable. Suddenly, the forest trail seemed smaller and the wooded area, darker. Her heart pounded in her ears. She saw nothing, yet the fear bubbling inside screamed for her to get out of there. She broke into a jog and burst through the end of the forest, stifling a scream. The large Victorian house stood before her.

The feeling of utter foolishness enveloped her. The call from Ryan must have brought paranoia. The only way to stop it was to contact the police. With a decision made, she strode purposely for her room to make that call.

Trenton stood in the woods. It had been a knife through his heart to see such terror cross Jayla's face. He wanted nothing more than to speak to her and ease her fears, and since he knew there was no physical way Tristan could have been there in the woods at that moment, he should have acted. He ached to hold her, yet instead, he watched her utterly terrified and scared of something.

Anger overcame him, and he strode toward the cottage. He needed to get her away from there so he could be himself. The pull to be with her was stronger, and he wavered in his desire for revenge. Could he let it go, convince Jayla to return to her life and allow him to be a part of it? He could walk away from The Cliffhouse and Tristan, couldn't he? He shook his head, knowing it was impossible. He hadn't spent the last sixteen years waiting for the right time, just to walk away because of a few emotions a woman evoked in him.

Disgusted at himself, Trenton pushed any thoughts of Jayla from his mind and made his way to the cottage to go over the plan once again. He paced around the living room, and thoughts of her reemerged. The woman was like a drug, and after touching her, he wanted more and more.

He groaned.

Maybe fresh air would help.

He stepped out onto the porch and stood at the railing. The very spot he had kissed her. He closed his eyes and could taste her lips, feel her looming presence. He slammed his hand down hard on the railing. What was the matter with him? How could she control his every thought? He had to see her again. Where had she had gone when she ran from the woods? Only one way to find out.

He started for the main house. If she wasn't in the rose garden, he would bide his time in the west wing.

seventeen

Jayla stared at the ocean with the phone in her hand. She needed to do this.

The phone rang, and she jumped. Another unknown number. "Hello?"

"Where are you, babe?" Ryan's voice cheerily came through.

Jayla could feel his smirk through the line. "What do you want, Ryan?"

"You, of course. Come home and let's discuss this."

"Home? My apartment is not your home."

His chuckle sent shivers down her spine. "Since when did you get so outspoken, my dear?"

"Since you trashed my apartment. Leave me

alone, Ryan. I mean it, or I'll call the police."

"Come on, Jayla. You know you don't mean that. I'll let you go for now, but I will find you, at which time we'll sit down and talk about this nonsense."

She hit the *End* button on the phone, then wrapped her arms around herself. This couldn't be happening. Cell phone in hand, she turned from the window. She needed to calm down in order to call the police. The rose garden was exactly the spot she needed to be. Not many of the other guests visited it. She could have privacy there to make the call.

She slipped downstairs and out the door, not running into Tristan. Only when she entered the garden did she take a deep breath. She was drawn to the lavender rose bush Tristan had pointed out. Since that moment, she had been more aware of the fragrance and beauty of it.

Her hand shook as she touched the petals and inhaled the scent. Tension left her and the trembling in her hand slowed. She leaned into the blossom and breathed the sweetness of it.

"One of your favorites now?"

She jumped around at the sound of the deep voice. "You startled me." She stepped back as Tristan walked toward her.

"I'm sorry. Didn't mean to. I've seen you at that bush more than the others since the day you were introduced to it."

"The scent is so strong and sweet."

"I didn't mean to intrude…"

"It's okay. I was just going to make a call, but it

can wait." She moved to the bench and sat. "Did you want to sit with me?"

"I'd love to." He glided to the bench, and she caught her breath at the flex of his thighs as he sat next to her.

"I've been thinking about the cottage." Jayla played with the cell phone.

"The cottage?"

"I didn't know if you would consider renting it out. I could use the quiet for writing, and then I could stay for the full summer. I'd be able to cook my own meals."

"Well, that's an interesting idea. I never thought of renting it." The corners of his lips turned up in a smile. "We might be able to work something out."

"Really?"

As he stood, he brushed a stray hair from her forehead. "Yeah, really. Let me get back to you about that."

"Thanks."

"I'll let you get to your call." With a wave, he headed out the arbored entrance.

Trenton moved toward the wooded side of the property. No sign of anyone. He was pushing his luck by seeking her out, but he couldn't help himself.

He chuckled. Jayla renting the cottage intrigued him. That would get her away from Tristan, and he could see her more. He warmed to the idea, his mind whirling to find a way to make it work without Tristan knowing.

He still needed to find a way to get her to the cabin. It was the only place he could be sure Tristan wouldn't show up. Trenton was playing with fire, and his concern for Jayla being burnt spurred him into finding a way to talk to her.

The garden felt so empty after Tristan left. Jayla looked down at the phone in her hand. She had no desire to go home at all. The sound of the ocean, the rose garden, and the peacefulness she felt there had filled the emptiness in her. With determination, she pulled out her phone and dialed information to get the number for the police station in her town.

The ringing in her ear resulted in a rising panic. What if he had anticipated this?

"Wentworth Police Department, how can I direct your call?"

"I need to speak to someone about being stalked." Jayla's voice trembled. There was no turning back now.

"You feel you are being stalked, ma'am?"

"Yes. My ex-roommate trashed my apartment before he moved out, and now, he keeps calling me. He's sitting outside the apartment."

"Can you see him?"

"I'm not there. I went out of town on vacation. He says he's there waiting for me. Please, how do I stop this?"

MIRRORED DECEPTION

"Hold one moment. Let me get a detective for you." The hold music was filled with static. She paced between the bench in the garden and the lavender bush.

"Ma'am, I'm Detective Reynolds. How can I help you?"

"I think I'm being stalked."

"Let's start with your name, shall we?" His gentleness calmed her.

"Jayla Ralston."

"Jayla Ralston? Are you aware your sister filed a missing person's report on you? Where are you right now?"

"What?" Panic rose.. Was Jenna worried that much? She should have called her. Jayla's mind raced.

"Ms. Ralston?" The detective's voice broke through her thoughts.

"Yes, I'm here. I had no idea my sister would do that. I haven't talked with her other than sending her a brief text about going on a mini-vacation."

"Hold on. Let me pull that file."

Jayla sank onto the bench as she waited for the detective to return. She knew without a doubt she had to call Jenna, but the question of how to keep her location a secret plagued her.

"Okay, Ms. Ralston. Can you let me know where you are now?"

"Is that necessary? I'd rather just find out how to stop Ryan from stalking me. I'll call my sister. Please disregard the missing person's report."

"Ma'am, are you there at your own free will?"

"Yes, of course. I told you, I simply took a mini-vacation after Ryan trashed my apartment."

"Okay. Let's start from the beginning. Who is Ryan and what happened?"

Jayla relayed the story from when Ryan moved in, up until she asked him to move out, and then finding the state of the apartment.

"Why didn't you call us at that time?"

"My sister was worried, but I just wanted to get away. So, I left."

There was a pause, and she could hear a tapping in the background. "So, the apartment is in the same condition as you left it?"

"As far as I know. I can arrange for you to get in if you would like to check it out. One of my neighbors has a key for emergencies. I can call her to open it for you."

"That would be helpful. Now, if you could give me a description of Ryan, I'll check out around the apartment as well. I'll need a number where I can reach you."

Jayla gave him her cell phone number. "I'll call my sister today."

"I'll leave that to you. I have no need to contact Jenna. Once I'm finished with the investigation of the apartment break in, I'll call you with an update," the detective reassured.

eighteen

Jayla sat on the bench, staring into space. The reality that her sister thought she was missing sank in. She had texted her, but Jenna never responded. Determined to wait until she heard back from the detective, she tucked the phone into her pocket.

It was becoming easier and easier to distance herself from the life she once knew. The more she wrote and stayed tucked away, the more she desired to remain that way. Deep down, she knew it was cruel not to call Jenna, but she just wanted freedom, to be out from under her sister's constant hovering, like she was an invalid and incapable of making decisions. Granted, she had made some *bad* decisions, but didn't everyone make mistakes?

Jayla shivered as a tingling started at the base of her neck. She slowly glanced around, but saw no one. She stood and forced herself not to hurry out of the garden. The sensation of being watched was strong. Having felt that a lot lately, she attributed it to paranoia because of the mess with Ryan.

Once out of the garden, the sun warmed her cool skin. She moved toward the house, intent on grabbing her purse and heading into town. Two steps up the veranda stairs, she paused and stared intently at the wooded area that led to the cottage. Would Tristan let her rent it for the rest of the summer? It was just what she needed—complete independence without the feel that she was running away. It would simply be a summer vacation for her.

Her face flushed at the thought of the kiss that was shared on the porch. *So amazing ...*

"Jayla?"

She glanced up to find Tristan standing at the top of the stairs.

"Sorry. Guess I let myself daydream." She continued up the last of the stairs and stopped beside him. "I was thinking of going into town. Is there a bookstore there?"

"Yes. At the very end of Main Street is Book Ends. It's owned and run by Ruth McKinley, but be prepared to stay a while, especially if she finds out you write. She'll talk your ear off."

"Great. I can't wait to meet her." Jayla went to get

her keys and purse. Within minutes, she was driving alongside the ocean view, her sister and her stalker forgotten for the moment. She entered Main Street and was taken aback. The town obviously hadn't changed much since it was established. Worn signs with fresh paint greeted her as she drove past them. She bet some of the stores had been there forever.

She parked in front of Book Ends and sat there for a moment imagining what it would be like to do her first book signing in a small place like that—homey, friendly. She pulled herself to the present and exited the vehicle. She paused outside, viewing the window display. Children's books took up the front of the left side. The right was full of suspense, romance, and more.

A bell rang as she opened the door and stepped into air conditioning. The store had the feel of oldness and newness wrapped into one. She wandered along the displays looking, picking up a book here and there.

"I'll be out in a moment!" a voice called from the back.

"No hurry. I'm just looking." Jayla was drawn to a corner in the back filled with beanbags and cushions scattered about. A rocking chair sat in the corner.

"That's our story land corner. The kids come and sit, and are taken wherever their imagination lets them go."

Jayla turned to find a petite, elderly lady with pure-white hair. The glasses she wore were perched on the edge of her nose.

"It's perfect."

"I have even found an adult or two curled up in those bean bags, reading." She winked. "Name's Ruth McKinley."

"Hi. Jayla Ralston."

"New to town or just visiting?"

"I've been staying at The Cliffhouse a few weeks and was hoping to rent a cottage for the rest of the summer."

"I wasn't aware there were any cottages open for the rest of the season. Those book up quickly around here."

"Oh, this is a private one."

"So, why do you want to hide away all summer in this rundown town?" Ruth laughed as she sank into the rocking chair.

Jayla slid into one of the beanbags and sighed. "I'm trying my hand at writing a children's book. It was easier to find a nice quiet place than try to do it at home."

"Hmm. House full where you live?"

Jayla played with the bottom button on her blouse. "No. It's just me."

She felt Ruth's eyes upon her. "Well, I'm sure if you put your mind to it, your book will be written." Relief flooded through Jayla the instant Ruth spoke. "How's that coming for you?"

"Oh, good." With a gush, Jayla launched into the plot and how she enjoyed the writing and getting carried away by the characters and story.

Time quickly passed..

MIRRORED DECEPTION

"Goodness!" Jayla apologetically stood. "I had no idea I took up your whole day."

"Dear, that's absolutely fine. This old store doesn't get much use anymore, and it's always a pleasure to have someone new to visit with. I do hope you'll come again." Ruth grasped her hand and squeezed. "I'll be dying to know how that book is coming."

"Thank you so much. I definitely will be back." On impulse, Jayla gave her a hug and headed for her car.

She reflected on how easy Ruth had been to talk with. She sighed. Ruth would be about her mom's age—if she'd lived. How she missed having her mom around to talk to. She would have understood about Jayla's desire to write. That thought warmed her. Despite her sister insisting she had to have a *respectable job*, Jayla suddenly remembered her mom's point of view. Jenna's thoughts definitely came from their dad.

Jayla realized she was more like her mom than she had thought about in a long time. Her mom had pushed herself to reach her goals and dreams and had wanted her girls to do the same. But once her parents died, Jayla had lost the confidence in doing much of anything—especially striving for her goals.

nineteen

The sun rose, shining bright through the large bay windows. Trenton sat in a newly uncovered chair in the cottage. He had spent the night cleaning, ready to offer it to Jayla to rent. Timing would be everything. He needed to get her away from The Cliffhouse to tell her the truth.

Memories flooded him as he looked around at the dust-free room. The cottage was the only place he felt at home when he was little, more so than the B&B. The little house wrapped him up in love and security, which was ripped from him once his father was killed.

Satisfied with the condition of the cottage,

he rose and climbed the stairs to the bedrooms. A ten-minute power nap was what he needed before he went in search of Jayla. He had to figure out how to get her checked out without Tristan knowing. The plan formed as he drifted off to sleep.

Trenton woke with a start and familiarized himself with where he was. He glanced at his watch. Only an hour had passed. Jayla would be starting for the garden if she was going to be writing today. She had been gone most of the day yesterday.

He straightened the covers on the bed and visualized Jayla lying there. The urge to be able to lay down with her was strong. Breathing deep, he tried to quiet the feeling. He shook his head and walked out of the room. It was time to ask Jayla to go away with him to the cabin.

With any luck, she would be moving into the cottage when they returned, hopefully once she knew the truth. He ran through the plan over and over again as he made his way through the wooded path toward The Cliffhouse. He paused in the shadows before the clearing.

People were sitting on the veranda, chatting. With a growl, he moved down the length of the clearance until he was at the back of the house. As no one was in sight, he sprinted to the entrance of the west wing. He needed to find out where Jayla was, so he entered the secret passage and quickly moved to her room. He slid the door open to look through the tapestry and saw an empty room. Cell phone was lying on the bed, laptop on the dresser. She wasn't writing in the garden after all.

He moved from room to room, peeking through the hidden holes in the tapestries to try and locate her. The living room was empty, as well as his brother's room. Frustrated, he turned and started back to the west wing.

In a moment of frustration, Jayla left for a walk without her phone. She didn't want to be held hostage to hear details about her past life and the relationship with Ryan. With a shudder, she considered what a terrible mess it could have been if she had been home when Ryan returned enraged. She felt extremely lucky to have come home after he had already left the apartment.

She walked along the main road. The exercise had cleared her mind. She stopped at the driveway entrance to The Cliffhouse, thinking back on the few short weeks she had been there. She had changed. She pictured a different life, one she used to have, as she wandered up the winding drive. There was nowhere else she wanted to be. This had become home. Her one regret was that she couldn't bring herself to call Jenna. She was sure her sister would get the message from the detective that she was no longer missing, but Jayla had yet to hear back from him.

She stopped on the lawn when she was about half way to the house. She wasn't the only one with secrets. The old Victorian held secrets, too; she just knew it. There was more to the past that happened there than Tristan had let on, and she wondered what the story was. Curious, she scanned the west wing. It was always dark and empty. She had a desire to explore it, but instinctively knew Tristan would never allow it.

Hmm…

Would he know, if it was open and she just let herself in?

Determined to embrace her newfound adventurous spirit, she moved toward the back of the building on the west side and glanced over her shoulder as she reached for the door. She twisted the knob. It wasn't locked. Her heart pounded in her ears.

She froze at the sound of laughter coming from the front of the house. Tristan's voice rang loud and clear as he talked to the guests.

She quickly walked around the house and into the rose garden. There would be a time when she could poke around the west wing. She sighed as she sank onto the bench. She didn't want to upset Tristan, but curiosity had won, and she couldn't resist.

Trenton tensed when the doorknob turned. His chest tightened in anxiety. Who would be trying to come in?

He moved to the hall, ready to slip into a closet if the door opened. A sigh of relief slipped out as the person moved away. He had no idea how much longer his presence would be unknown there. He needed to get Jayla away to tell her the truth before he was found out. He was tired of living a lie. He wanted his life back— and he wanted it *now*.

Twenty

Ryan hung up the phone. He turned to the computer and replayed the recording he had just made. Quick key strokes focused in on the background noise from his conversation with Jayla. Seagulls? He leaned back in the chair, and stroked his chin, then pulled up Google and searched for hotels and motels along the coast in a 100-mile radius.

He removed ones that he knew would be out of Jayla's price range and narrowed the search further. He shook his head; none of them were Jayla's style. He changed his search pattern and looked for bed-and-breakfasts and country inns. Not as many, but three right on the coast. He'd start there. His first instinct told him she would go south along the coast. Only one in that direction, so that would be his first stop. If need be, he could spend the night there, and then head north. Hopefully, his instincts were right.

He packed a small bag, threw his laptop in another—along with his small recorder—and headed for the door. He glanced over his shoulder around the small apartment he had leased since leaving Jayla's place. Unpacked boxes still littered the floor. With a shrug, he turned around, determined he would find Jayla, and she would come to her senses.

In no hurry, he enjoyed the scenery as he drove, playing and replaying through his mind how Jayla would react when he found her. Surely, she'd be over her snit by now.

He'd been driving for an hour. The first place he checked had been a bust. He headed north to check the other bed-and-breakfasts on his list. One was off the beaten path, and the other on the main coastal route. If she was trying to hide, she would have gone off the main road. He steered the car in that direction.

He beat his fingers on the steering wheel in time with the music. He had let his temper get the best of him, yet he softly cursed, thinking of Jayla calling the police. Once he found her, he'd convince her to come home, then teach her to leave their problems unsaid. Why did she have to start acting like Maggie all of a sudden? Maggie had caused such problems for him, and now Jayla seemed determined to do the same.

Fury ran through him.

MIRRORED DECEPTION

Time quickly passed. Before long, the side road leading to his second stop appeared. Over the next twenty minutes to the bed-and-breakfast, he formed a plan.

Ryan scanned the cars in the driveway as he pulled in. Jayla's wasn't there.

He exited his car and looked around. The house was run down. A vacancy sign hung, listing to one side. The lawn was overgrown.

"Need a place to stay?"

Ryan turned at the young voice behind him. "I was supposed to meet my girlfriend, but left the directions at home. Can you tell me if she's here?" He pulled a picture of Jayla out of his pocket.

The teenage girl looked, shaking her head. "No single women here. Could be at The Cliffhouse farther up the coast."

"That was the name. Thanks." He grinned as the thought of surprising Jayla crossed his mind.

The summer season was in full swing. The B&B was occupied and Jayla had hardly seen Tristan the past few days.

Although she was relieved to avoid the subject of their kiss, she missed the interaction between them. Writing in the rose garden had become her daily practice. Today, however, she sat on the bench just staring at the flowers, her laptop idle beside her.

The night before, the detective had called and

talked at length regarding his encounter with Ryan. He felt Ryan had moved on, but they were running patrols past her building on a regular basis to watch for him. Detective Reynolds told her if Ryan tried to contact her, she was to let him know immediately.

She felt better knowing her apartment was being watched, but guilt pangs hit her as she assured the detective she would be in touch with Jenna and again, didn't make the call. Jenna would find out that Jayla was alive and well sooner or later when she checked on the progress of the missing person's report. If she called, they would assure Jenna that her sister was just away on a short vacation. The phone would start ringing like there was no tomorrow when that happened.

As had become routine for her, she knew a walk would clear her head. She moved toward the entrance to the garden as she thought of which direction to go: the cliff walk, the wooded trail, or the road. Deciding on the road, she turned and ran into the B&B to put the laptop in her room before heading back outside. She drew in a deep breath on the veranda and deliberately let it out slowly.

She moved down the stairs. No one was around. It was a quiet day. Earlier, Jayla heard people talking about going to the local beach. She was halfway down the drive when Tristan stepped out from behind a tree.

She stopped short. "You scared me."

"I didn't mean to. I'm sorry." He stepped aside and gestured. "Go ahead. Want some company?"

She searched his face. Which personality would

she be dealing with today? Her stomach clenched in anticipation when her eyes met his and found only warmth shining from them. "Of course. I'd love it."

He reached for her hand. They walked in silence hand in hand for a time, then he cleared his throat. "I've been thinking about the cottage. I don't mind renting it to you, but before you move in, I'd love to take you away for the night. Do some antiquing. Take you to my family cabin. Really have a chance to spend some time with you."

"I don't know what to say." Jayla's mind raced. "When were you thinking about doing this? I know it's your busy season, and with The Cliffhouse full, I wouldn't think you could get away." Should she be nervous about wanting to be alone with him?

"I have a good friend that will stay for one night and handle things. It'll be fine." He squeezed her hand. "I think we should just keep it to ourselves, not mention it in front of the other guests. Why don't we meet at the cottage?"

"That sounds intriguing…why not?"

"Good. Pack an overnight bag, and drive your car over to the cottage. We can leave it there while we're gone. When we get back, I'll help you move the rest of your stuff."

"Sounds like a plan." Her heart skipped a beat at the thought of being away with him and at the added excitement of having the rest of the summer to herself at the cottage. She could really get some writing done and be completely independent. A win-win situation.

Jayla spent the rest of the walk quizzing him about the cabin and the area in which they would be antiquing. Laughter and banter were easy between them, and Jayla relaxed more and more. *This* was the man who sparked her into awareness. If only they could maintain the easy way together instead of lapsing into the cordial, business-like exchanges that were so awkward and void of emotion.

After making an excuse in order to leave Jayla at the end of the driveway, Trenton continued walking to the cottage. He ran through the rest of his plan, mentally checking off things that were falling into place. His stomach flipped with anxiousness at the thought of telling Jayla the truth. He needed to free himself from the lies, but the fear of losing her paralyzed him.

There were still so many answers he needed. Why did his father have to die? Why was his childhood ripped from him? How did his mother die? The whys that plagued him always brought a surge of anger. Jayla calmed him and made him want the answers for different reasons. When he was with her, revenge wasn't on his mind. Instead, he wanted answers so that he could move forward with his life, a life that included Jayla.

Memories of his childhood flooded back as he walked up the driveway for the cottage. He'd spent time with his dad at both the cottage and the cabin.

Good memories consumed him. Memories that had been cut short when his life ended. Ended in a way that he would never forget, resulting in a black cloud of events and places he *wanted* to forget.

A headache started again. The pain was always associated with the awful reality of his childhood. He needed to see a doctor at some point, but now all his focus was on getting Jayla to know the truth about him and hopefully forgive his lie.

Twenty-one

Ryan stood in the shadows, watching the house. Jayla was on the veranda, talking with another couple. He scowled as she laughed. He moved deeper into the shadows before turning on his heel and returning to his car parked down the road.

He slid into the driver's seat and pounded the steering wheel. She needed him, and he would make sure she knew it. He turned the engine over and drove toward town, forming a plan. Before she knew it, she would be running home—home to be with him.

He pulled into the back of the motel where he had found a room. He made his way to it and settled onto the bed, then opened his laptop. He Googled The Cliffhouse and started digging. He'd seen the man Jayla was walking with, and also saw him in the woods watching the B&B the same as himself. He was sure there was more to that owner than met the eye, and Ryan was going to find the truth.

The first story he found was from sixteen years ago, talking about the death of the owner, Jeffrey Montgomery. It had been ruled an accident when he fell over the cliff. Mysteriously, two years later, the owner's wife was hospitalized for unknown reasons. Ryan grinned as he read the articles. Unexplained disappearances and deaths, now that was something he could work with. What would happen if Jayla disappeared? Did Jenna even know where her sister was?

The first article also mentioned the owner's two sons, twins. Ryan reopened the obituary for the wife. It only referenced one of the sons taking over the business. No mention of the second son. He stared into space as he processed this information. Another disappearance? Didn't anyone in the town question a missing son?

He grabbed his pad of paper and made a list of questions. The reporter hat was back in place; he knew a good story when he saw it. Ryan would make sure Jayla was gone from the B&B before he started nosing around. He loved a good challenge, and Jayla had proved to be just that.

He spent the majority of the night sifting through different articles and formulating questions. He paced the room, thinking of an excuse to get into

MIRRORED DECEPTION

The Cliffhouse. Ryan still carried his newspaper credentials even though he hadn't worked there for a year.

He stared out the window as his mind wandered to the past year. He had used his job to run background checks *and* stalk past girlfriends. Maggie had put an end to that. When he got caught, he was immediately terminated. He tried to talk his way out of it, but couldn't hide it. Thankfully, charges weren't pressed.

After losing the job at the newspaper, Ryan spent the next few weeks drinking on a daily basis. Jayla had been the one to bring him out of that. She gave him a place to stay and encouraged him to get out of the rut he was in. He immediately fell in love with her—her gentleness, kindness. He had believed in a relationship that didn't exist in Jayla's eyes. The last straw was when she kicked him out of the apartment. Ryan knew he could change her mind as soon as he was able to spend some alone time with her, away from her overbearing sister.

Ryan drove up the driveway to The Cliffhouse, constantly scanning for Jayla's car. Not seeing it, he parked. With a deep breath, he grabbed his pad and pen and started for the house. It was hidden from the road, allowing privacy for the guests. He smiled as he thought how Jayla would have felt safe there.

He ran his hand along the painted railing as he climbed the steps to the front door. The main door was open behind a screen door. He entered and took in the antiques in the foyer and beyond into the living room.

"Hi, can I help you?"

"I'm looking for the owner." Ryan twisted the pen between his fingers.

"That would be me. Tristan Montgomery." Tristan held out his hand.

Ryan firmly shook it. "Ryan Edmunds. I'm working on a piece for a regional paper about bed-and-breakfasts along the New England coast. Can I have a few minutes of your time?"

"Sure. Not certain what there is to tell. This has been a family-owned-and-operated business for decades. My dad ran it before me and his dad before him." Tristan gestured toward the dining room. "Would you like a cup of coffee?"

"That would be great." Ryan scanned the walls as they moved into the dining room, his glance resting on the view from the large bay windows. "Incredible."

"Definitely. I couldn't imagine living anywhere else." Tristan pointed at a table by the windows. "Have a seat. I'll get the coffee. How do you take it?"

"Black, please." Ryan drifted toward the table, watching the sea moving lazily with small waves coming in.

"So, what are you looking for exactly?" Tristan sat down with a cup of coffee for himself and placed Ryan's in front of him.

"Well, the piece started out about bed-and-breakfast places, but as I've been going along, I've discovered that many of them have their own little story. I find them fascinating." Ryan sipped from his coffee. "I'm hoping to get the story that makes your B&B what it is today."

Tristan glanced out the window at the cliff walk. "There really isn't a story here."

"Come on. Every old house like this has a story. A ghost roaming about, hidden treasure from years ago, unexplained disappearances?" Ryan took another drink of coffee.

Tristan chuckled. "I don't know what it is you're looking for, but there's no ghost story here. Quiet family-owned business, that's about it."

"Okay. Can you explain the death of your father? I understand it was ruled suicide, yet there were a lot of unanswered questions."

Tristan swallowed hard, shaking his head. "I was nine when he died. I honestly don't know the details. It was suicide. Is that really the story you're after?" Tristan stood.

"I didn't mean to offend. I just have found, through my research, that there seems to be a mystery lurking here in the house. It really could help boost your business." Ryan gestured for him to sit down.

"There's no mystery, and I'm full every season. Really don't need the help boosting my business." Tristan continued to stand. "I think we're done here."

Ryan rose from his chair. "One more question. Can you explain the disappearance of your twin with no obituary or missing person report filed?"

"What? My brother died when we were ten. I

had lost my dad, and the next year, my brother. What are you searching for?" Tristan clenched his hands at his side.

"I'm a reporter. We look for stories. I'm sorry if I offended you." Ryan picked up his pad of paper. "Great coffee, thanks. I'll let myself out."

Ryan made his way to the front door, his mind searching for a way to find the rest of the story. He would have to head to town.

Tristan watched the back of the car as the reporter headed down the drive. Unanswered questions? What was he trying to dig up? He shook his head to clear the doubts snaking through his mind. Did Trenton really die? If not, why would their mother lie about it? In the end of her illness, in her delirium, she talked about wanting forgiveness from Trenton. Tristan always assumed it was out of guilt because she didn't get Trent to the hospital in time when he was ill. He never questioned it, figuring she was delirious and just a heartbroken mother riddled with guilt about the death of a child.

He mentally filed away a note to go through his mother's old things in the west wing. He didn't want to find any stories lurking that he wasn't aware of, and he certainly didn't want to read about them in the paper.

Twenty-Two

Jayla threw some clothes into her smaller bag. She had no intention of checking out of The Cliffhouse, but when Tristan asked her to go antiquing and spend the night at a family cabin, she could not resist the curiosity to see if the spark so often electrified between them could sustain if they could get away alone.

If she found some good antiques, hopefully it would soften Jenna's reaction to the fact that a simple text was her only contact.

Which side of Tristan would Jayla see on this venture? Her mind wandered to the mystery surrounding him.

She grabbed the bag and rushed to the car. Tristan had told her to meet him at the next house up the road. With everything she needed stowed in the trunk, she cautiously drove the car into the driveway of the carriage house.

As she parked, she saw him on the porch, leaning against the stair railing. Butterflies moved through her stomach as her eyes swept down the length of him. The jeans snug against his hips brought a soft sigh across her lips. Muscles flexing, Tristan pushed away from the railing, and Jayla mentally berated herself, knowing she needed to get a grip.

She got out of the car. "Are we taking my car?"

"Of course not." He pulled back a tarp covering a motorcycle. "Feel free to hold on."

Jayla stared at him; mouth slightly open. He was walking toward her, holding out a helmet.

"I don't know about this." Her voice trembled.

"It's okay. I'll be careful." He extended the helmet once again. "Like I said, feel free to hold on." His eyes twinkled with laughter.

He loaded her overnight bag into one of the side saddlebags. She gingerly held the helmet, eyeing the bike. This was exactly a situation Jenna would discourage.

Jayla straightened her shoulders and slipped on the helmet. "Ready when you are."

Tristan started the motorcycle and helped her on. She wrapped her arms around him, praying he couldn't feel the heavy pounding of her heart.

They started down the road, and Jayla relaxed.

As she enjoyed the view, she mindlessly slid her hands down to Tristan's thighs and comfortably rested them there.

He pulled into a small town and parked the motorcycle. Jayla got off the bike. She lifted the helmet from her head and dangled it from the chin strap, then spun in a circle. The town was full of antique shops, many of them having items outside their doors, crowding the sidewalk.

"Wow, look at this place! My sister would have a field day here." Jayla turned toward Tristan. "Jenna is an antique dealer and loves to find new stuff."

"Well, let's look around. Then the next time you see her, you can share this hidden treasure with her." He reached for her hand, drew it to his lips, and brushed a soft kiss against her palm. "If I tell you how to find it again."

"Oh, that was mean." Jayla pushed him away and started down the sidewalk. She heard him chuckling behind her as she headed for the first shop. The door was wide open. This particular store had no antiques outside, so she stepped in and was transported to a different time. Foot-powered sewing machines, butter churns, and hand-roller washing machines were scattered about, as well as other old furniture topped with porcelain pitchers and basins.

She made her way around the room, running her hand over the old wood, tracing scars of the past. She could understand her sister's love for the old relics.

"There are lots of stores to go through, if you want. Or we can stay here and you can daydream all day."

The sound of Tristan's voice brought Jayla from her thoughts. "I just wonder what the stories are in these pieces of furniture. Look at this one with the long scar down the center, all jagged like. Can't you just imagine what caused it?"

"No wonder you're a writer." He grabbed her hand and led her to the door. "Let's see what treasures you can find in the next store."

They spent the next few hours wandering from store to store with Jayla inventing stories for different pieces. Nearing the end of the street, she spied a small ice cream shoppe. She grabbed Tristan's hand and headed for the treat shop. His fingers intertwined with hers, and she felt giddy, thinking about him and the cabin. The constant awareness of chemistry between them gave her hope that this was the true man she had seen glimpses of before.

With cones in hands, they sat near the window to watch people walk by. Jayla watched Tristan with half-closed eyes as she lazily licked her ice cream. He kept his eyes on her tongue as she took a slow lick, running her tongue over her lips to catch any drips.

"Keep that up and we won't make it to the cabin, Jayla."

She tried to keep a straight face. "Whatever do you mean?"

She widened her eyes at him as he leaned forward and licked the other side of her ice cream. His face close to hers, she couldn't keep her eyes off him. She lowered the ice cream and moved forward. Tristan's lips barely touched her, and she shuddered

MIRRORED DECEPTION

as his tongue moved over her mouth like a feather.

"You almost ready to go?" He sat back with a smirk on his face as he looked into her eyes, *his* smoky with desire. "We still have a bit of a ride ahead of us."

Jayla cleared her throat. "Of course." She looked down to see her melting ice cream run down her hand. "I would say I'm done. You?"

"Just getting started." He stood and held out his hand to her.

She couldn't keep the smile from her face as they were once again on the motorcycle headed for the mountain cabin.

Twenty-three

Jenna drove up the driveway of The Cliffhouse, shaking her head. No way would Jayla be in such a place. It was too secluded.

Jenna left her bag in the car, got out, and stretched. She'd been on the road for hours and had stopped at every hotel along the way. No one had seen Jayla. Frustration had been mounting, and she was getting more and more exhausted with every mile that went by.

Jayla had been gone for three weeks, and Jenna had had enough. She'd been to the police to report a missing person, but they didn't believe anything had happened to her. They'd questioned Ryan Edmonds, and he admitted to trashing the place but said he hadn't seen Jayla before or after he left it. Jenna wasn't sure she believed him, but the police had. They told Jenna there was nothing they could do unless evidence proved foul play had been involved. The police had also let her know that Jayla had called and assured them that she was on vacation.

Jenna decided to go out on her own to look for her. This bed-and-breakfast certainly didn't look like the type of place Jayla would stay, but Jenna needed a room for the night, then she would start again in the morning. She slowly took the steps up the porch. *Where could Jayla be?*

Jenna knocked on the door and waited. The house was an old Victorian and well kept. She went into *business mode* and wondered how many antiques she could find inside.

"May I help you?" The man at the door looked her up and down. "Jayla?"

"No, I'm Jenna, but you know my sister? She's been here?" Jenna was floored. She grabbed a recent picture of Jayla from her purse and shoved it at the man. "This is Jayla. Was she here, and if so, when?"

"Yes, that's her. Wow, you two are identical." He grinned. "You must hear that a lot."

His smile unnerved her, and her eyes overflowed with the emotions she'd been holding back for the last three weeks. Jenna couldn't believe it. She'd never cried in front of anyone.

"Hey, are you okay? Come in. I'm Tristan." He reached for her hand.

Jenna stepped forward and collapsed against him. He wrapped his arms around her and gingerly held her.

"I'm sorry. I'm not sure what came over me. I'm usually so much stronger. I've been looking for her for three weeks now." Jenna sobbed through her tears.

"It's okay. Come on in. How about some tea? Coffee?"

"A cup of tea would be great." Jenna wiped her tears. "I'm so sorry." She walked away to look out the window and collect herself. "So, is Jayla here?"

"She has been, although she doesn't appear to be now. Her things are still here, so I'm sure she'll be back soon."

"Then she can't be far." Jenna finally had hope…

"I would assume so."

"Do you have any rooms available? I'd like to stay until she gets back." Jenna took the teacup Tristan handed to her. They had moved to the living room where she perched on the edge of the couch. She couldn't believe Jayla had been staying there all this time.

"I'm full this week." Tristan looked at her with compassion. "I'm sure Jayla is fine."

"You don't understand. Her apartment had been broken into, and then all of a sudden, she disappeared. The police wouldn't do anything, and I haven't heard from her. I'm worried about her. I need to be here when she gets back—if she *does*. I'm not convinced she's fine." Jenna's voice cracked as she held back the tears.

"I can let you stay in the room Jayla stayed in. That's all I have this week."

"I'll take it." Jenna smiled. "Thank you."

"I understand. I do. She was pretty relaxed the whole time she was here—I can tell you that. She worked a lot on her laptop, and we had some great conversations. She's a wonderful person. She enjoyed my mom's rose garden and spent a lot of time out there." Tristan reached out and covered Jenna's trembling hand. "I'm sure she's okay. She probably just went on a day trip to do some sightseeing."

Jenna sipped her tea. "I suppose we'll just have to wait and see."

"How about we get you settled in her room? Do you have a bag?"

"It's in the car. I'll go get it." Jenna placed the teacup on the end table and stood. "Tristan, do you really think she'll be back?"

"I do. You'll see." He stood as the telephone rang. "Finish your tea, and we'll get you settled in a few minutes."

Jenna watched him head to the front desk. She sank into the couch and picked up her tea. Her thoughts went to the conversation with the detective who told her the missing person's report had been closed. She'd been furious when he said he had spoken to both Jayla and Ryan. She wasn't convinced that Ryan wasn't involved in Jayla's disappearance, and she had even expressed to the detective that she believed Jayla had not called the police on her own free will. The detective had been quick to assure her otherwise, but Jenna just wasn't convinced.

The tea grew cold as she stared into space. Jayla had changed so much since their parents died. Jenna had tried to keep an eye on her; maybe she had been too protective. Was Jayla running from her? Could she be trying to distance herself?

Twenty-four

Jenna had spent a sleepless night in Jayla's room. She'd gone through her laptop looking for clues as to where her sister might have gone. She came across the book Jayla had started writing and was impressed at her sister's obvious talent. Jenna had spent the night tossing and turning, wondering why Jayla had never shared her dream of authorship with her.

She had also found notes jotted down about a local bookstore and the owner, Ruth McKinley. Jenna was determined to start there that morning to see if Ruth knew where Jayla might be.

Showered and dressed, Jenna walked downstairs. Fresh coffee and homemade breakfast pastries were waiting. People were scattered about the dining room, making plans for the day. She helped herself and moved to a corner table by the window. She picked at the pastry as the waves rolled in. The sea had a calm about it—one Jenna wished she could feel.

"How'd you sleep?"

Jenna startled at the sound of Tristan's voice. "Not that great. Spent a lot of time going through Jayla's stuff. Did you know she's writing a book?"

"Yes, she writes every day."

"I had no idea. She never told me she had an interest in that." Jenna tapped her fingers against her coffee mug. "How can sisters be close and not know each other's deepest dreams and desires?"

"It happens. Sometimes, the people you're closest to are the ones that you most dread criticism from. Maybe that's why Jayla kept her dream from you."

"I hovered over her, you know. I suppose she probably felt smothered. But she had a tough time when our parents died. I didn't want to lose her, too." Her voice broke with emotion.

"Maybe you did hover, but I'm sure it was out of love. Did you ever consider your sister is stronger than she appears?"

"I guess maybe she is. Maybe I needed her to lean on me."

Tristan stood. "Give yourself a chance to just think and relax. Enjoy the area here as Jayla enjoyed it the past three weeks. Look at life through her eyes for a bit and perhaps you can connect with her again on a different level."

Jenna stared after Tristan as he walked out of the dining room. Had they grown so far apart by her playing mom to Jayla instead of just being her sister? With a sigh, she stood. Hopefully, she'd find more answers in town at the bookstore.

On the way into town, a peace overtook her. The soft sound of the ocean in the background eased her tension. She drove down the main street, amazed by the quaintness of the setting. It was exactly the kind of place Jayla would love. *Homey.* Somehow, it brought memories of their mom. She was always ready for a new adventure to seek out small towns and learn the history of them. She felt a small town told a story. Jenna realized that Jayla had a lot of that in her also. How could she have been so blind to not see Jayla growing into the same type of person as their mom had been?

She pulled into the closest open spot and exited her vehicle. The sidewalks bustled with tourists. Shop doors opened and shut. Jenna closed her eyes and inhaled deeply. The smell of the ocean heightened her senses. The salty scent and cool air engulfed her. She opened her eyes and glanced down the street. Book Ends was just down the sidewalk. She crossed the street and headed directly for it. Her starting point.

The window display was quite well done. She immediately felt a connection with Jayla there. Their mother had taken them to the library and bookstores as children and had instilled a love of reading. A small bell rang as she opened the door. She slowly moved around the shelves and tables, reminiscing of times her mom had taken them to bookstores.

"Jayla?"

Jenna turned to see an elderly woman watching her. "I'm her sister, Jenna. You know Jayla?"

"Oh, my. You two certainly look alike, don't you? Yes, I know her. She spent some time here, kept an old lonely lady company one day. Such a sweet dear. I'm Ruth, by the way."

"Have you seen her lately?"

"No, dear. Why do you ask? I believe she's staying at The Cliffhouse." Ruth gestured toward the chairs in the corner. "Come sit down and tell me what's got you so concerned."

Jenna slid into a beanbag. "I don't know. She left home a few weeks ago with no word. There'd been an incident at her apartment, and I was worried about her. The police don't seem concerned, but it's not like her to not answer her calls."

"I'm sure she's fine. She's been very busy with her writing."

Jenna clasped her hands together. "Yes, so everyone keeps saying."

Ruth watched her. "Did you not know about her writing, or do you just disapprove?"

Jenna lifted her head, and a lone tear ran down her cheek. "I don't disapprove, but apparently, she thought I would. She never told me."

"Ah. Well, sometimes sisters can't tell each other everything. Have you shared all your hopes with Jayla?"

"No, but I was the one that took care of her…"

"Took care of her? You two are the same age. You should be sisters…the best of friends…not a mother-daughter act. I'm sure she's okay, dear. Jayla is a big girl who can take care of herself. No reason to fret."

Jenna nodded. "I suppose. But I just can't help feeling there's more to it. Something strange is going on, and everyone just expects me to believe she's fine just because they think so."

"Have you checked with Tristan at The Cliffhouse?"

"Yes, he says she's okay, but doesn't know where she's been the last day or two. He's not even sure when she left, but her stuff is still there."

"Well then, she can't be far."

Jenna stood. "Thank you for your time." She headed for the door and waved goodbye.

"Good luck, dear!" Ruth hollered after her.

Back on the sidewalk, Jenna started walking with no particular destination in mind. The smell of freshly baked sweets stopped her in mid-stride and she turned into a small diner. The waitress was filling a multi-layered pie server with three, freshly baked pies.

"Sit wherever you like."

Jenna slid onto a stool at the bar. "A slice of the apple, please." When it was placed in front of her, she sighed with contentment at the first bite. Her mind, for a brief moment, forgot her sister and just remembered memories of her childhood and her mom.

Twenty-five

Jenna finished her pie and left money on the counter. She started for the door, giving a glance around to the almost-empty diner. She stopped with her hand on the door handle, staring at the man on the street. It couldn't be!

She flung the door open and ran outside. "Ryan?" She hurried over to him.

He gaped at her. "Um, Jenna? What are you doing here?"

"I'm looking for Jayla. Where is she?" Her shrill, angry voice demanded an answer.

"I don't know."

"Liar! I want you to tell me." She firmly grabbed hold of his arm.

"Jenna, please stop making a scene. I have no idea where she is." Ryan tried to pull his arm away, but she held on.

"Someone help me! Call the police!" Jenna looked around as people passed by. "So, *you'd* better help me, Ryan. Come clean on this. You better not have hurt her."

"I'd *never* hurt her." He jerked free from her grasp as a police cruiser drove up.

The officer got out of his vehicle and approached them. "Is there a problem, ma'am?"

"Yes, officer. My sister has been missing for three weeks and this man has been stalking her. He won't tell me where she is."

The officer eyed Ryan. "Sir?"

Ryan sighed. "I don't know where she is. She left our apartment three weeks ago, and I've been looking for her. Her sister is just upset because I didn't let her know where I was looking."

"What a liar!" Jenna scowled at Ryan, then faced the policeman. "Officer, this man was *kicked out of* my sister's apartment three weeks ago, and he trashed the place upon leaving. Jayla has been missing ever since." Jenna held out a business card. "This is the local detective on the case. Please call him."

The officer took the card. "I'm going to ask both of you to come to the station with me while we get this straightened out."

"I'll follow you. My car is parked right there." Jenna spun on her heel and headed toward her car.

"Sir, would you come with me, please?" The officer gestured toward his car.

"Certainly. You'll see this is all a big misunderstanding." Ryan settled into the vehicle and leaned back. His mind raced with possible ways to get out of the situation. If the cop talked to Detective Reynolds it would not look good for him.

The air was stifling, and he suddenly felt boxed in. His hands became clammy. His mind raced with how he could talk his way out of this one. He knew he wasn't in the wrong for anything. All he did was care about people and it always came back to bite him in the ass.

They arrived at the station, and the officer escorted Ryan into an interrogation room, then left him alone. Ryan paced around the room. He tended to get claustrophobic and this room wasn't much bigger than a closet. He could feel perspiration on his forehead and he braced himself against the wall to focus on breathing. Could anxiety be a defense? He took a deep breath and tried to spin an excuse where anxiousness overrode his common sense. Nah, that was no good.

Jenna eagerly told the officer everything she knew. He finally gestured for a female officer to bring her some coffee.

"I need to make a phone call," he said as he headed from the room. He paused at the door and looked back at Jenna. "I'll be back as soon as I know something." He walked out holding Detective Reynolds' card.

Jenna sat there sipping the bitter brew. The station was fairly quiet. Small, with very few staff available. With a sigh, she turned toward the window. Jayla had to be out there, but where? What could Ryan have done with her? She shuddered at the thought that Jayla was lying somewhere hurt, or worse.

"Ma'am?" The officer waited for her to turn. "I spoke with your detective. I have a few questions for Mr. Edmunds, and then I'll be back to talk to you. Just sit tight for a little longer."

"Take all the time you need. I'm not going anywhere without information on my sister."

He gave a brief nod, then walked away. She pulled out her cell phone and the number for The Cliffhouse that Tristan had provided. Her nerves jumped with every ring of the phone.

"The Cliffhouse." Tristan's deep voice immediately filled her with relief like the voice of an old, comfortable friend.

"Tristan, it's Jenna."

"Hey, what's going on? Everything okay?"

"I'm at the police station. I ran into Ryan in

town. The police are questioning him about Jayla's disappearance."

"Jenna, we don't know that something has happened."

"I'm aware of that, but she's been gone for three weeks with no word from her. You say she was fine, but now even you don't know where she is. Ryan has been stalking her since she kicked him out."

"Okay. I hear you. Wait and see what Ryan says before jumping to conclusions. Do you want me to come down there?"

Jenna took a deep breath. Was this the reason she called him? "Would you?"

"Sure. I'll be there in a few minutes."

"Thanks." Jenna sat down. Her knees felt weak, and the energy was drained from her.

Since when did she need a man in her life to make her feel safe?

Now, maybe?

She closed her eyes and rubbed her temples, relieved to know someone would be there with her… just in case.

Ryan shifted in the chair once more. "I'm telling you I don't know where Jayla is. Maybe she's running from her overbearing sister."

"I spoke with the detective who asked you to stop sitting outside her apartment. Why are you here? Did you follow Jayla Ralston?"

"I didn't even know for sure she was here. I've already told you numerous times, I don't know where she is. I'm writing a story on bed-and-breakfasts and went to interview the owner of The Cliffhouse."

"Very convenient since that's where she's been staying." The officer sat back in the chair and crossed his arms over his large chest. "I have all day. We can sit here until you're ready to talk."

The officer watched Ryan, tapping his fingers on the table. "The other detective did a little digging after he told you to stop sitting in front of Jayla's apartment. Any clue what he might have found?"

"I'm sure nothing that's against the law." Ryan shifted in his seat.

"Really? Ironically, they found that you have an outstanding warrant for stalking and violating a restraining order."

"Charges weren't filed."

"Quite the contrary, Mr. Edmunds, you had a court date and skipped town. Looks like you'll be joining us for a little bit until we can reach the proper authorities to come get you." The officer stood. "Sit tight for a few more minutes, I'll be back."

The door quietly shut behind the officer. Immediately, Ryan shoved his chair out and stood. He clenched his fists at his sides.

This is ridiculous!

He needed to get out of there and away before something was pinned on him. *This isn't good*. He paced the small room until the officer came back.

"Well, Mr. Edmunds," the man said, "you'll be

taken to booking now and into a holding cell." He stood back as another officer came in.

"You have the right to remain silent …" the man droned.

Ryan tuned out the dreaded words, and once the officer finished rattling them off, Ryan reluctantly allowed him to lead him from the room.

Jenna was pacing the hallway when Tristan arrived. "Are you okay?"

Jenna nodded. "Thank you for coming."

Tristan pulled her into a hug and held her briefly before stepping back. "Any answers yet?"

Before she could speak, Jenna heard the door open and she watched Ryan being led away. She stood as the officer walked toward her. "Did he say where Jayla is?"

"No. Unfortunately, he isn't saying anything about your sister. However, he is under arrest for an outstanding warrant for violation of a restraining order after stalking a female."

"What? When was this?"

"A few years ago. He's not going anywhere right now." The officer handed her his business card. "I'll keep in touch if we hear any more. I suggest you call the local detective that you filed a missing person report with. He may have more information for you."

Jenna turned toward Tristan. "What does that mean?"

"Let's head back to The Cliffhouse, and you can call him and see."

Twenty-six

Jenna turned the car toward the coast and headed back to The Cliffhouse. She parked next to Tristan's and laid her head on the steering wheel.

Tristan knocked on her window and she lowered it. "I just need a minute."

He nodded. "Take your time. I'll be inside."

With her eyes closed, she fought the urge to dissolve into tears. She needed to be strong, but she was at the end of her rope. She exited the vehicle, straightened her shoulders, and started inside. The day wasn't over, and yet, she was ready to crash.

The smell of fresh coffee assaulted her as she walked into the foyer. She followed the scent to the dining room and found Tristan pouring himself a cup. He reached for another cup for Jenna, and poured her a cup of tea from a small teapot next to the coffeepot.

"So, now you call the other detective?"

"At this point, yes." Jenna set the mug aside and looked at Tristan. "Tell me more of what Jayla was like while she was here."

He sat back in his chair and looked out the window. "I would find her in the rose garden a lot, writing. She enjoyed her coffee, always inhaling the scent with her eyes closed before taking a sip." He smiled.

"She always did like coffee much better than I do."

Tristan looked at Jenna. "You two really aren't identical, except in looks. Jayla was so reserved, and yet her zest came through when she was interacting with other guests, and especially when she was writing."

"Really? I always thought Jayla had no aspiration for anything. She just seemed to go through life without much enthusiasm since…our parents died."

Jenna's cell rang. "Hello?"

Tristan sat and listened to half a conversation as he watched the ocean. Since Jayla had been there, he had found a new love for the sound and scent of it. He admired her, but felt no chemistry for her. He often caught her staring at him and wondered what was going on in her mind. Sometimes, she almost looked puzzled.

"That was the detective back home," Jenna said. "He spoke with Jayla a few days ago, and she assured him she was fine. She also asked him to close the missing person file. She promised she would call me."

"Well, that's a good sign. She's obviously not missing."

"Then why hasn't she returned my calls? I've tried for three weeks to reach her, and she won't answer and won't call me back." Jenna played with the mug.

"I don't have the answers for you, Jen." Tristan reached for her hand and covered it with his. "While we wait for her to come back, how would you like to check out the rest of the house? I think I may have a few antiques you'd be interested in."

"More?" Jenna's interest sparkled in her eyes.

"Yeah, the whole west wing. It's been a while since I've been there, but I promise you it'll be worth the trip. What do you say?" Tristan squeezed her hand. "Later today if you want."

"I'd love to. I'll need my camera."

"Give me an hour, and then we'll go over." Tristan pushed back his chair.

"Sounds good."

Twenty-seven

he wall tapestries of wool, the rich textures... Jenna sighed. She couldn't find that quality around very often. She wanted to make him an offer for one of the tapestries, as she knew she could resell it immediately. In fact, she knew just the buyer, but Jenna had a feeling Tristan would never sell.

She rounded the corner in the staircase and stopped short. Tristan stood at the bottom, talking to a young couple at the front desk. She raised her camera and took pictures of him signing them out. His masculine jaw was softened by his lopsided smile.

His laughter reached his eyes; happiness was sincere across his face. He made his guests welcome with his sincerity and warmth. She could see why Jayla had immediately fallen in love with the place. Now if they could just find her.

Jenna leaned against the wall on the landing, and her mind wandered to her childhood when she and Jayla would explore and be gone for hours, paying no mind to their mother's calling. She smiled, remembering how mad their mother would get for being ignored by the two of them. Was Jayla off on an exploration now, or had something happened to her? Her car was nowhere to be seen, yet some of her stuff had been in her room—her laptop, her large suitcase—certainly giving the impression that she was coming back.

"What's that smile about?" Tristan came lightly up the stairs.

Blinking to the present, Jenna grinned. "Was I smiling? I was thinking of Jayla."

"She couldn't have gone far." Tristan leaned against the wall. "I know you're a photographer, but why the need for a camera?"

"I thought we were going to the west wing to look at antiques. I like to have my camera with me in case I come across anything unusual. I hope you don't mind." Jenna gave a sweet smile.

Tristan chuckled. "Of course not. Ready?"

They rounded the corner of the house, and Tristan filled Jenna in on how the west wing had been the servants' quarters when he was a kid. Main-ly, *old* Sam had lived there with a few others. Sam was the gardener who had been really a good friend of his mother's. It wasn't until Tristan was older that he had suspected that his mother had had an affair with Sam.

"Here we are." Tristan opened the door and stepped aside to allow Jenna entry. "It's probably extremely dusty. I don't think anyone has been in here in years."

Jenna first noticed the living quarters. The couch had pillows strewn about. "Is this how things were left?"

"I don't remember. I haven't been here for about ten years. This wing holds some very sad memories."

"You don't have to share if you don't want to."

"No, it's okay. I don't want to upset you."

"Actually, I'm interested. My mother used to say that every person, place, and thing had a story. I'd like to hear your stories."

"I usually don't talk about it, but like I said, I haven't been here for a decade. I didn't realize it would have such an effect on me. Sam killed himself when I was sixteen. Took a gun to his head outside on the cliff walk after he had been drinking and fell off the edge. No one really knew why. We all assumed it was because my mother had died in the hospital."

"Why was she there?" Jenna asked, watching Tristan with wide eyes.

He walked around the living room, straightening pillows on the couch. "She never was quite right after Trenton died when we were ten. He was my twin. She got worse and worse, mentally. I finally couldn't take care of her. It was just she and I. The doctor recommended putting Mom in a mental facility."

"I'm so sorry."

"No…I'm sorry for being so heavy. I don't normally share all this with people. Enough about my life story." Tristan cleared his throat and started for the back of the house. "If I remember right, upstairs there were some really old pieces."

He led the way up to the first bedroom and stopped at the doorway. "Someone's been here." He gestured to the duffel bag next to the bed.

"Whose is that?"

"I have no idea." He bent down and started shuffling through it. An old picture fell out—one he recognized of himself and Trenton when they were nine. "It can't be. Who would have this picture?"

Jenna snapped photos of the bedroom and the duffel bag. "What are you going to do?"

"I don't know. Let's look around some more. It's obvious they're not here now." Tristan started searching through the closet and bureau.

"I'm going to look in another room." Jenna moved to the next room, a smaller bedroom. In a corner sat a small trunk. She snapped pictures from all angles before looking in the closet and drawers. Finding nothing, she moved to the trunk. She took a deep breath as she opened it.

Inside were photos of twin boys she assumed were Tristan and Trenton playing in the rose garden. In most of the pictures, a man stood in the background, watching them. Jenna set the photos aside. Halfway down the trunk was an old, black diary. She pulled it out. Should she read it?

No, it wouldn't be right.

She set the diary aside, dove farther into the trunk, and found a packet of old letters addressed to Sam from Tristan's mom. "Tristan!"

He rushed into the room. "Did you find something?"

"This old diary and some letters. Do you want to look at them?" Jenna held the diary out to him.

"It must be Sam's." He pointed at the pictures. "That's Sam there. He was always around when we were kids."

"Do you think you should read this?"

"I don't know. It might be interesting." Tristan sat on the bed and opened the blue cover. "The first entry was shortly after he came to work here, I know because it was right about the time Dad died."

Tristan skimmed the first few pages, then tipped his head and turned the pages much slower. "Jenna, these entries are the days before Trenton's death."

"What do they say?"

"He talks about Trenton being the evil one. How could he say that about Trent? He goes on to say how much better off Mom would be if she didn't have to put up with such a terrible son and just had to concentrate on raising me." Tristan concernedly looked off into space.

"The day Mom told me Trenton died," Tristan continued, "Sam wrote, *I did it. I took that evil child away. They won't find him now. I told Anna that the boy has gone to be with his father. She knows what I mean."* Tristan's eyes darkened with anger. "I know what he means, too. I overheard him talking one night in his drunken stupor. He said he had killed my father when he first came here in a fit of jealous rage. My mother was so in love with Sam she never told anyone. She protected him."

"Oh, God, Tristan. You're kidding. Are you sure you heard right? If he was drunk…"

"I'm sure that means he killed Trenton. No wonder my mother went insane." Tristan threw down the diary. "It's a good thing Sam killed himself. I would have killed him myself if he was here."

"What else does he say?" Jenna reached for the diary.

"I don't care. I don't want to know."

Jenna thumbed to the page where Tristan had left off. She skimmed over it and continued on. "He didn't kill him, Tristan."

"What?"

"It says right here. *I took the boy food yesterday and he was belligerent. Tried to escape. Told me Tristan would come get him.*"

"Where did he have him?"

"It doesn't say." Jenna looked up. Tristan paced the floor. "Should I keep reading?"

"Yes!" Tristan sat and held his head in his hands, staring at the floor.

"It skips a few days, and then says he moved the boy. Doesn't say where. Says he makes him work for his food, feeding animals. Must be on a farm of some sort. Talks about him being no better than the pigs. Oh…"

"What?"

"He goes on to say that he didn't do what he wanted him to do, so he whipped him, *badly* the way he describes his back afterward. Says it was torn up pretty bad from the whip."

Tristan grabbed the diary and read the page. Tears filled his eyes. Jenna wanted to hold him, to soothe him. "How could he have done this? Trent was a child."

"Tristan, I'm sorry."

Tristan scanned the next few pages. The hope in trying to find good news amidst this nightmare. "Look, the entries stop for a while. The next entry is dated four years later. He talks about moving Trent again. This time he says he moved him to Rockport. That's not far from here."

"He had to stay close if he was still living here and going back and forth."

"Trent would have been about fifteen then. Jenna, this is only about a year before Sam killed himself." Tristan started reading quickly, turning pages faster.

Jenna laid a hand on his arm. "Are you ready to know what really happened?"

He looked up at her. "I have to know." He practically flew through the pages and suddenly tapped on one in particular. He pulled her to sit beside him on the bed. "Look right here. It's the date before the suicide. He writes, *I went to see the boy again. He is getting stronger every day. He knocked me over when I got there and before I knew what happened, he was gone. I don't know what to do. What if he goes to the police? He knows I killed his father. He saw me, which is the reason I had to take him. The brat was asking questions and telling me he was going to turn me in. I should have done away with him when I had the chance, but I just couldn't bring myself to do it. I know how much his mother loved him."*

Jenna put her arm around Tristan. "What now?"

"He's out there. Trenton is alive. Sam took my brother from me all those years ago. He forced my mother to go insane thinking her son was dead. I not only lost my brother, but I lost my mother that day, too."

"Where do you look for him?"

"Sam had stuff in the carriage house. Let's start there. Maybe we'll find a clue in his things."

He threw all the pictures in the trunk and closed it up, then grabbed the diary, and they ran down the stairs.

"Where's the carriage house?" Jenna asked.

"It's through the woods a ways. We used to play there as kids, but after Trenton died—or was *taken*—I never went back there."

Tristan took Jenna's hand and guided her onto an old, overgrown path. At least they could see it well enough to follow it. At the edge of the woods, a small cottage stood in a clearing. Parked in front of it was Jayla's car.

"Why is her car here?" Jenna broke free from Tristan and ran forward.

"Wait!"

Jenna ignored him and pulled on the door handle. It was locked. Inside was Jayla's sweatshirt.

Birds chirped in the trees as Tristan and Jenna reached the porch of the house. They started across to the door. The floorboards creaked. Jenna screeched as a mouse ran in front of her.

"It's just a field mouse." Tristan laughed. "You okay?"

"Just a little spooked. Where is Jayla?"

"I don't know why her car would be here, but not her. Stay on the porch, and let me look inside." Tristan searched around while Jenna stayed on the porch.

Tristan joined Jenna on the porch. "Nothing, although it looks like it was just cleaned. There are even fresh flowers on the table."

Jenna stepped down a few steps, intending to sit on the stairs.

"What is that?" Jenna pointed at a tread mark beside Jayla's car.

"Looks like a motorcycle tire. My guess is maybe she went off with someone."

"Someone else who was possibly staying in the west wing?" Jenna demanded.

"Jenna, I don't know." Tristan ran his fingers through his hair. "Let's go have some dinner, talk about this, and see what we can come up with. There seems to be a lot of stuff going on, and I don't know if any of it is related."

"Is there anywhere else Trenton would have gone? Could it have been Trenton in the west wing?"

"I don't know. He would be the only one who would have that picture of us as kids." Tristan gazed upward as if in deep thought. "The cabin."

"Cabin?"

"My dad had a cabin. It's a four-hour ride. Up on a mountain. Trenton used to love the place. I haven't been there for years."

"Well, what are we waiting for? Let's go check it out." Jenna starting running for The Cliffhouse.

"Jenna, wait! Let's make some definite plans!"

"We can make them in the car!" Jenna called back over her shoulder. "We don't have time to waste. If Jayla is there, I want to find her!"

In no time at all, Tristan was jogging right beside her, and they soon arrived back at The Cliffhouse.

"I need to make sure Devan will cover for me while we're gone," Tristan said. "We won't be able to leave until morning. I don't think I can find it in the dark." Tristan left Jenna in the foyer as he headed to the kitchen to make arrangements.

When Tristan came back from the kitchen, Jenna was pacing. "Okay, we are all set. Devan can cover. Let's meet here in the morning at five? That would put us there about nine, give or take."

Jenna gave him a quick hug before starting for the stairs. "That sounds good!" she threw over her shoulder.

She closed the door behind her. The realization of being so close to Jayla hit her, and she sank to the floor, tears streaming down her face. Where was she?

After a decent cry, she wiped her tears, stood,

and wandered around the room. She stopped at the window and gazed out at the ocean. A calmness washed over her. Jayla loved the ocean, and Jenna understood why her twin wanted to be there.

With a sigh, she turned and reached for Jayla's laptop. She waited for it to boot up, her mind wandering to the past. Tristan's story—his father, brother and childhood taken from him—made Jenna and Jayla's trivial squabbles seem just that, *trivial*.

Jenna opened the file for Jayla's story. Within minutes, she was engrossed. Intriguing and riveting, Jenna never looked up until she finished reading to the end. She set the laptop aside and crawled into bed, more determined than ever to find her sister and support her and whatever she chose to do.

Twenty-eight

The road was windy and narrow. Jayla clung tightly to Tristan's waist as they hugged the curves on the motorcycle. She loved the feel of the bike on the *open* road, but the snaky mountain road made her very nervous. She trusted him to handle it, but her heart raced with every turn he took. She rested her helmeted-head against his back and moved her body with his as one.

They had spent a quiet evening in another small town. Tristan had been a gentleman, insisting on two rooms. Jayla sighed. With all the teasing, she had been anticipating more, but on some level was glad he was going slow. He was so intriguing and had an air of mystery around him. At least he was being consistent.

The motorcycle slowed, and he turned it left onto a dirt driveway. The path was barely wide enough for a car to pass through and looked like it hadn't been used in years. Jayla shivered a bit. What had she had gotten herself into? She hated to admit she was notorious for not having the best judgment. She shoved the thought out of her mind.

A cabin stood at the end of the lane. Though small, Jayla could see it was well kept. The motorcycle came to a stop, and Jayla was slow to dismount. Her legs were weak from the ride.

She walked beyond the cabin and her breath caught at the sight. She could see for what had to be miles below. It was like she could touch a cloud if she reached straight out beyond the mountaintop.

"It's breathtaking." Jayla turned to see Tristan watching her.

"It certainly is. I've loved this place since I was a kid." He walked up to her and wrapped his arms around her. "I couldn't wait to share it with you."

"What now, mountain man?" Jayla laughed at his grimace.

"Mountain man?"

"I'm from the city. I know nothing of what to do up on *these here mountains*." She laughed as she went to grab her overnight bag. "But I'm thinking my makeup probably needs refreshing."

"I think you look better without it." Tristan scowled.

"What? You can't be serious?"

He grabbed her hand. "I'm very serious. Jayla, you're beautiful without makeup. You don't need it, so just forget about it, and let's take a walk through the woods."

"Are you crazy? What about animals?"

"There isn't anything up here that's going to bother you." He laughed. "Except maybe me." He pulled her close and nibbled along her neck.

She softly sighed. Almost instantly, his kiss became demanding, yet gentle, as he found her lips.

Jayla pressed herself against him, carried by her own response. She matched her passion with his and teased him with her tongue.

Tristan groaned and pulled away, while she tried to catch her breath.

"Let's take that walk." He grabbed her hand and turned toward a path in the woods.

The splendor amazed her. "Wait! What's that?" She ran, following the sound, and stopped in a clearing where a waterfall cascaded over the ledge. The late sun glistened off the water, giving the impressions of diamonds running down the rocks. "Wow. How did you stay away from this all these years? This is almost as great as sitting and listening to the ocean."

"I know. I had forgotten over time how wonderful it was. It certainly has a calming effect, doesn't it?" He pulled her close, and they stood wrapped in each other's arms, mesmerized by the water.

"I could fall in love with this place," Jayla whispered.

"We could always go for a swim."

"I don't have a swim suit." Jayla blushed.

"Maybe another time, then." Something tentative lay in his eyes, and he seemed almost relieved that she'd declined.

"How about some dinner?"

"Dinner? Now?"

He laughed. "You do realize hours have passed, and it's about four. I'm starving." He started for the house, leaving her to stare after him. Something she'd come to relish doing.

She got her feet moving, and they returned to the house. Tristan went inside, gripped the edge of the sink, and closed his eyes.

Jayla stood in the doorway, watching him. "Tristan? Are you okay?" Clearly, he was suffering some sort of inner struggle. Should she ask about it?

No, not now.

It disturbed her to see that the *other* Tristan had returned. At times, it was like she was dealing with two different men. Sometimes he was gentle and caring, and at other times, exciting and edge-of-the-seat dangerous. She loved the dangerous side of him. Yes, she could admit to herself that she loved him, but could she tell him? For a fleeting second, he looked so sad, almost tortured.

"I'm fine. Just a little headache. I'm just hungry." He started to gather the steaks for grilling.

"Let me help." Jayla prepared the salad and rice

as he grilled the steaks in silence. Her mind was a whirlwind. She lit a couple of candles for the table and finished setting the plates for dinner. "Everything's ready here." She poured the red wine.

They ate in silence. His eyes were dark and stormy, and he scowled most of the evening. After three glasses of wine, she couldn't stand it anymore. "What happened? Tristan, what's going on?"

"We need to talk, Jayla, I just don't want to do it right now." He got up and stormed out the door.

She cleared the table and did the dishes. What on earth happened between the passionate kisses they shared overlooking the waterfalls and now?

With a sigh of exasperation, Jayla grabbed a book and headed for the bedroom. A quiet night of reading might be the thing to do. She read for hours. She glanced at the clock to realize that it had gotten quite late. She turned out the light, figuring she would see Tristan in the morning.

The bedroom door flew open, startling her awake. She glanced at the clock. *Two in the morning.* "Tristan? Is that you?"

"Are you expecting someone else?"

"What are you doing?"

"I'm here to finish what we started."

"Not now. It's the middle of the night." Jayla turned on the light beside the bed and found Tristan leaning against the doorframe. His jeans were unbuttoned and his shirt hung open.

"We only have the weekend. Why waste time? You're not really going to turn me away, are you?"

"Have you been drinking?"

"Nope." He wandered closer to the bed.

She had very little on and tried to pull the covers up, but Tristan was quicker and yanked them back. "Hiding from me?"

"Not like this, Tristan."

"Like what, Jayla?" He kneeled on the bed with one knee, and put his hands on either side of her. Softly, he kissed her on the lips, then playfully nipped her bottom lip. He pulled back and looked her in the eye. "Like what?"

"Tristan," she whispered, yet her voice trembled.

"Yes?" He lightly ran his tongue over her lips. "Tell me you want me to go away, and I'll go." He tenderly kissed down her jawline to the curve of her throat. A soft moan escaped her. "Does that mean you want me to stay?"

"Yes."

He chuckled as he pushed her back against the pillows, the weight of him on top of her, his mouth claiming hers. She ran her hands under his shirt and up his back. Her fingers traced ridges there.

"Tristan? What…?"

"Later, Jayla. Questions and talking later." He reached over and turned off the light, then got up, stripped his clothes off, and slid into bed beside her.

She trembled as he gently removed her camisole. He ran his hands over her skin, groaned, and pulled her close.

Twenty-nine

The alarm went off at four-thirty and Jenna reached out to hit it. She had only a few short hours of sleep, but she jumped from the bed, reaching for clean clothes. She hoped Tristan was as ready to go as she was. She didn't want to waste another minute.

Downstairs, she found Tristan dressed in snug jeans and a form fitting T-shirt. His dark hair was unkempt, yet not messy. Her breath caught, and she released it slowly. She had never been so instantly attracted to a man.

She picked up the pace as he turned toward her, his lopsided grin greeting her. "Ready?"

"Absolutely. You said four-hour ride?" she questioned.

"Give or take, depending on traffic. Hard to say for sure with the tourist season in full swing."

They started off. Adventure awaited around the corner. Jenna's stomach fluttered in anticipation. She needed to see Jayla, to know that she was going to be okay. Would they find what they were looking for?

Jayla awoke to find her bed empty. She stretched and smiled. *What a night.* She could smell bacon cooking downstairs and heard Tristan whistling.

She threw on some yoga pants and an oversized T-shirt. She brushed her teeth before pulling her hair back in a ponytail, then paused at the mirror, deciding against makeup.

She skipped downstairs to greet Tristan and stopped short at the bottom. What would she say to him? She had questions, and he'd said they needed to talk, but she didn't want to just jump right into it.

"Coffee ready?" She smiled shyly.

"You bet, and breakfast is almost, too. I didn't think you were ever going to get out of bed." He drew her close and softly kissed her. "Good morning, beautiful."

"Good morning." She poured her coffee and sat down. "Do you want some help?"

"Nope, all under control."

Jayla walked to the deck and enjoyed the view while replaying last night in her mind. *His back...* "Tristan?"

"Yeah?"

"What happened to your back?" She could see his reflection in the sliding door. He never missed a beat cooking, but a look of panic briefly crossed his face. For a second, Jayla thought she imagined the fleeting expression. She remembered seeing him working in the rose garden and taking off his shirt. He hadn't had any scars on his back.

"It's ready."

She turned to face him. "Are you going to answer me?"

"It's not worth talking about. It's from my childhood. Something I would just as soon forget."

"Tristan, I think we have something good between us, and I hope you're able to be honest with me." She sat at the table and started filling her plate. She was trying to keep her face neutral, but every nerve in her body was screaming for her to run. Something was very wrong.

"Jayla, do you trust me?"

"Yes. Have you given me reason not to?"

"There's something I need to tell you." The rumble of an SUV coming up the driveway had them turning toward the windows.

Tristan jumped from his seat and ran to the door. "Are you expecting anyone?"

"Of course not. Who would I be expecting?" Jayla watched as he searched around the living room.

"What are you looking for?"

"There used to be a gun here."

"A gun? For what"

"I don't know who's coming. I want to be prepared." He seemed almost frantic now.

"What is it that you're not telling me?" Jayla grabbed him by the arm. "Tell me now!"

"Jayla!" a familiar voice shouted from outside.

"Jen?" Jayla ran for the door and paused when she saw her sister. "Jenna! What are you doing here, and… Is that Tristan?" Jayla faltered. "But, if you're with Jen, who is…?" She turned to look inside the kitchen again.

"Jayla, I was trying to tell you." *Tristan* pleaded as he crossed the foyer and reached for her.

She backed away. "Stop. Don't touch me. I don't know who you are."

"Trent?" The *other* Tristan stepped forward. "My God, it's you! I thought you were dead."

"I bet you did," Trenton grumbled, then turned and walked in the house. He came back out with his helmet in hand. "You've had all these years to have everything. I'm back, and I'm claiming my half."

"Have what I wanted? Trent, I wanted my brother. I was told you died when we were ten. We just found the diary of old Sam and figured out what really happened. I had no idea."

Jayla stood with Jenna and watched the exchange between the brothers. Jayla couldn't believe her eyes! She only knew Tristan. Who was this other man named *Trenton*? It was like looking in a mirror, a mirror of deception.

"Can we just get out of here, please?" Jayla moved onto the porch, her arms crossed tightly across her chest.

"Jayla, please. Let me explain." Trenton stepped toward her. "Give me a chance to at least talk to you."

"I think you've had your chance. You could have told me last night, instead— Oh, my God, instead…"

"Jayla, please."

"No, Tristan, *Trenton*, whatever your name is."

The real Tristan took a step forward. "Trenton, give her some time. We *all* need it. Come back to The Cliffhouse, in the house, not the west wing."

"I prefer the west wing."

"Fine. But come back so we can talk this through." Tristan studied his brother. "I can't believe it's you. I've missed you so much." He cleared his voice, his struggle with his emotions, evident. He reached out for his brother, stopping short when Trenton backed a step.

Trenton's eyes searched his brother's as if he wanted to believe him. After several long, drawn-out moments, Trenton frowned and shook his head. He got on his motorcycle and drove off without a backward glance.

Jayla watched him until he disappeared, then turned and hugged her sister. "How did you find me?"

"I had no idea what happened to you. Why would you just take off like that, after your apartment had been broken into? Are you nuts?" Jenna spoke with a hint of anger, but Jayla recognized even more concern.

"I just wanted time to myself—away from everything."

Tristan started in the house, pausing next to Jayla. "I'm so sorry this happened. We can talk later, but I'll be inside for now so you can have some time with your sister."

"Jayla, I was worried sick. When I got your text saying you were going away for a vacation, I figured you would head for the beach. I waited to hear from you again, but when you ignored my calls, I got scared. I decided to search every hotel on the coast until I found you. I finally came across The Cliffhouse. It was the most unlikely spot I would think of for you, I must say."

"Which was why I chose it." Jayla laughed. "I'm glad you found me when you did. I can't believe any of this."

"We certainly found more than we had been looking for! I kind of had my suspicion about Trenton after Tristan let me into the west wing to look at antiques there, and we came upon the diary of the old gardener, who apparently was the one who kidnapped Trenton when he was ten. Long story short, it led us to the carriage house where we found your car, and Tristan then remembered this cabin from when they were kids. So, we decided to look here."

"Kidnapped him?" Jayla stared at her sister. "I didn't know that. God, that must have been awful." She shook her head. "He led me to believe he was Tristan all this time. I was falling in love with him." Jayla sighed as she walked across the grass and looked out at the view. "I know, always picking the wrong guy."

"I don't think you picked the wrong guy, Jayla. I'm not saying he did the right thing. But you fell in love with him, not Tristan. He couldn't have been pretending to be someone else the whole time… what if the one you fell in love with was truly who he is."

"Maybe, but he was also dishonest. You can't build a relationship on that."

"Is that what you want? A relationship?" Jenna stood beside her.

"No. I was looking for excitement, and I guess I found it. Now it's time to go home and get ready for the new school year." A pain sliced through her at the thought of returning home.

"What about your book?"

Jayla turned to face her sister. "You know?"

"Yes. We found your laptop. Why didn't you tell me?"

"I didn't think you would approve. I know Mom and Dad wouldn't, and I can't stand it when you ask me, *what would Mom and Dad think?* Why does it seem like we have a hard time connecting lately, Jen? I miss my twin." A lone tear ran down Jayla's cheek.

"I'm so sorry, Jayla. Of course, I support you and your writing. If you write a children's book, I'll be your biggest fan. Honey, I know you can do it. And as far as Mom, you know she would've been there cheering you on. She would have loved an artist of some sort in the family."

"Thanks, Jen. That means the world to me." Jayla tightly hugged her sister and felt closer to her than she had been in a long time.

"Let's go home. I think Tristan has closed up the cabin and probably wants to head back."

"I just need to get my things." Jayla ran inside.

In the bedroom, she threw her stuff into her bag. She picked up the camisole from the floor and held it as she stared at the bed. Last night, *Trenton* had awakened a part of her she thought didn't exist. She threw the silky garment in the bag and closed it. Tears filled her eyes as the memories from their lovemaking flooded over her. She had needed him to stay with her. She hadn't turned him away when he'd given her the chance.

Jayla left the cabin, ran to the car, and threw in her bag. "Let's go."

Jenna and Tristan exchanged glances and got in. Jayla was silent as her mind replayed her night with Trenton over and over.

Thirty

Trenton's bike hugged every curve at speeds that would have been mind-boggling had he been thinking about it. He rode as one with the bike, yet his mind was elsewhere.

As he slowed and pulled to the side of the road, he had only Jayla on his mind. He had blown it. He never should have waited to tell her the truth.

He stared at the ocean. Where should he go now? It was time to face his fears and push through all the pain, and anxiety the years of being held captive had woven into his life. Jayla had given him a reason to fight to live—not for revenge anymore, but for love.

Yes, he loved her…

He turned his bike and headed toward the small town where he'd grown up. He had only one place on his mind. It was time to release some of those demons and face them head on.

With a definite destination in mind, his grip on the handlebars relaxed. He sat back and enjoyed the scenery while keeping a steady pace. Gone was the urgency to go fast and try to outrun the memories.

He slowed to a crawl as he turned into the open wrought-iron gated fence. He remembered the plot being in the back of the cemetery. He parked the bike to the side, removed his helmet, and walked toward the headstone. Smooth gray granite with the simple words of wife and mother under her name – Leann Montgomery.

Trenton kneeled in the grass in front of the grave. Fresh flowers had recently been placed. He wondered who would be so thoughtful.

"How did this happen? First you betrayed Dad, and then *me*?" Trenton set his helmet on the grass beside him.

"I blame you! Did you know I begged for you to come get me and that evil old man just laughed at me? You told Tristan I was dead. What kind of mother does that to her son? Didn't you have enough love for both of us? What kind of wife were you? What kind of mother? What kind of woman?"

He rubbed the smooth granite. A plethora of emotions coursed through his body. "I lost my whole childhood. How could you love a man who was such a monster? How could you have protected him after what he did to me, Mother? I was ten years old!"

Anger filled him as he stared hard at the headstone. This was the first time he had spoken the words that had fueled his anger for so many years. She had abandoned him. She continued to love Sam regardless of what he had done to her husband and son.

Tears that had never been cried burned his eyes as he struggled to hold on to the anger. Years of disappointment, hurt, and fear ran through his body, and he broke down.

In the beginning, he had held onto hope that someone would rescue him. All those years of crying out for his brother, and no one showed. Sam had taunted him with how well Tristan and his mother were getting along so much better without him. The truth had hit Trenton hard.

The pulsing anger that fueled his teenage years and young adulthood needed to be released. As an adult, he could fathom the reasons no one had come for him, but the lost childhood plagued him. He resented the choices he had to make through the years that molded him—choices he should have never been forced into.

For years Trenton lived alone, surviving on anger and hurt. Now Jayla had taught him he could be loved. The one thing that mattered the most to him he had lost forever. Hatred for his mother surged again.

He ripped the fresh cut flowers from her grave and tossed them away. Hands clenched at his side, he softly cursed. Could he ever forgive her? He had a hard time even picturing her anymore. Good memories had faded over the years as the seeping anger took over.

With a sigh, he laid back on the grass. The clouds in the blue sky danced by at a leisurely pace as he replayed the past years. The memories were just that. Simply *memories*. More distant now that he was no longer fueled with fury. The one thought he couldn't shake now was the night with Jayla. The shared passion he thought would never be. Her love had done it, softened his anger and caused it to dissipate. Loving Jayla had set him free, and now, he had lost her.

He wiped the few straggling tears from his face.

Released from the pain and stress of carrying around his quest for revenge, he drifted into a comfortable doze. Suddenly, he felt a hundred years old. He slowly opened his eyes to see the sun setting softly on the horizon. "Mother, I can't say I forgive you, but I can say I'm not angry anymore. Can I really believe you didn't know? You stayed with Sam, loved him as you should have been loving Dad?"

Trenton grabbed his helmet as he stood. "I'm sorry you never knew me, or the man I turned out to be. I only hope Jayla wants to see that man. I love her, and I can't have you or Sam take that from me. My past will no longer have a hold on me."

He turned and strode away, slipping on the helmet. He straddled the bike and took one more look over his shoulder. "Good bye, Mother," he whispered as he turned his bike toward the road.

thirty-one

The ride back to The Cliffhouse seemed to take forever. Jayla's thoughts tumbled. The past weeks, her confidence had grown, and it all shattered at the sight of Tristan and Trenton together.

She'd had enough quiet and needed answers. "Was it you that offered me the cottage to rent for the rest of the summer?"

Tristan met Jayla's eyes in the rearview mirror. "I'm sorry, no. But if that's what you want, I don't have a problem with it."

"Were you ever at the cottage with me?"

"No. I haven't been there in years."

"The rose garden?"

"Yes, numerous times. Though I never wanted to disturb you, so I usually left shortly after you arrived." Tristan hesitated. "Jayla, whether you want to hear it or not, I think the memories you're referring to were all with Trent."

Jayla sighed and closed her eyes. How could she know who she had fallen in love with?

Jenna turned to face Jayla. "Do you want to stay the rest of the summer?"

"I don't know anymore. I wanted the peace to write, but now I'm not sure."

"Give him a chance to explain," Jenna said softly.

"Why? So I can hear more lies?" Jayla snorted in disgust. "I wouldn't believe a single word he said."

"Jay, there are things you don't know." Jenna glanced at Tristan.

"She's right," he said. "I had no idea Trent was alive, let alone the nightmare he had been through."

Jayla watched the scenery go by. "He thought you abandoned him and his mom...What *did* happen to her?"

"She died. She lost her mind after Trent was taken. Was never the same." Tristan's voice cracked with emotion.

Jayla watched her sister reach out and rub Tristan's shoulder. "You get a second chance with him. You just need to sit down and talk it through.

Many years have passed, Tristan, so it may take time." Jenna kept her voice low.

"I know. If he *will* talk to me. I don't even know how to get in touch with him."

Jayla shook her head at the obvious attraction Tristan and Jenna had for each other. She had felt that way with Trenton.

Her breath caught. She suddenly realized that every moment she was with Trenton she had come alive. She suppressed the urge to laugh out loud when she understood why she so often questioned why there seemed to be two different Tristans. Why couldn't she have seen it before? When she had spent time with Tristan, she had enjoyed his pleasant company, but when she had been with *Trenton*... he made her feel alive.

She leaned her head against the back of the seat and closed her eyes, then slipped into a restless sleep, remembering the feel of Trenton against her, holding her.

She missed him already.

thirty-two

Trenton parked his bike in the driveway. No more hiding. He pulled off his helmet and noticed Jayla's car parked in what had become her usual spot. Would she talk to him?

He huffed and faced the house. Lights burned brightly from many rooms. He turned toward the west wing. No need to sneak in anymore, but he wasn't about to go to the main house.

He flipped on the lights. He hadn't even thought to look for Sam's diary, which Tristan had found. He placed the helmet on the table and made his way to the couch. As he sank into it, his chest tightened at the thought of being alone – without Jayla. He had screwed up royally and had no idea how to fix it. If only their siblings hadn't come to the cabin when they did. He would've had a chance to tell her.

The pounding in his head started again. He sprawled on the couch and covered his eyes with his arm. He drifted to sleep, only to be plagued by the memories of holding her in his arms.

A knock on the door startled him awake. With a sigh, Trenton stood. It was time to face his brother—unless with some glimmer of hope it was Jayla. He swung open the door to find Tristan standing there. "I figured it was you."

"Hoping for someone else, though?" Tristan's eyes searched his.

"Doesn't matter really. Come in if you're going to." Trenton headed back for the couch as Tristan shut the door. "You don't actually want to have this conversation tonight, do you?"

Trenton lay back against the arm of the couch, feet sprawled in front of him. Tristan lowered himself to a chair across from him.

"What conversation? I'd like to talk, but you make it sound like some sort of showdown."

Trenton chuckled. "I suppose I do. Being on the defense has become second nature to me." He studied Tristan as he looked around the living room. "You act like you've never been in here."

"I hadn't since I was a kid, until yesterday. While

you were gone, I avoided places that brought back memories of you. It was just too painful."

Trenton leaned forward. "Tell me, Trist, just how hard of a life has it been for you since that night I was taken? Has it been really rough, because your life doesn't look too bad to me!"

Tristan stared at Trenton. "Hard in some aspects, yes. I know it was nothing compared to what you must have been through, but without my brother by my side, yes it was hard. I missed you every day. A part of me died that night."

"Let's assume for one second that you actually did miss me. Was life that bad—just you and Mother?"

"You really don't get it, do you? Mother was never the same. She went insane and ended up in a psych hospital after you disappeared. I think she truly believed you were dead." Tristan ran his hand through his hair. "Did you really believe all these years that Mom and I were just having a grand old time because you were gone? We lost Dad, and then suddenly, less than a year later, *you* were gone. Shortly after that, Mom was gone too, mentally at least." He sat back in the chair, frowning.

"I was ten when Sam took me. He whipped me and beat me daily, taunting me with how great you and Mother got along without me. What would you have believed if you were in my shoes? Did you know Sam killed Dad?" Trenton could barely get the words out.

"I didn't back then. I overhead Sam in a drunken stupor mumbling about it, but even then, I wasn't sure. By that time, Mom didn't even know who I was."

Trenton sat back and closed his eyes. His headache had intensified, and he just wanted to slip into unconsciousness to rid himself of the pain. He reached into his pocket and pulled out the bottle of the few precious pain pills he had left. He swallowed one without water, then glanced at his brother.

"Are you okay?" Tristan's face was etched with worry.

"Fine. A lingering effect of being hit by a shovel one too many times, I imagine. I guess at some point I need to have it really looked at, but for now the pain is worse when the memories hit me."

"We don't have to keep talking tonight if it's too much." Tristan stood.

Trenton waved him back into his seat. "Let's get this over with. I know it wasn't realistic of me to expect my ten-year-old brother was going to rescue me, but I *did* think you would be hunting for me, especially as I got older."

"I would have, if I thought you were alive. Trent, you have to believe that. Not a day went by that I wasn't wishing you were here."

"I was so bull-headed back then. You remember how I thought I knew everything? I saw Sam push Dad off the cliff. When they said he must have killed himself, I thought I could make Sam tell the truth if I told him I saw him. I never thought it through."

"You confronted him? *That's* why he took you."

"Yeah. I think Mom knew he killed Dad. Apparently, they had been having an affair for years."

"I just recently found that out, too. Why didn't

you tell me you saw him do it?"

"I should have gone to Mom. Maybe she would have done something." Trenton rubbed his throbbing temples.

Tristan stood and paced the floor. "Sam told Mom that he took care of you like Dad. I truly think Mom thought he killed you, too."

"Why did she stay with him? What kind of mother's love is that?" Trenton punched the pillow next to him and laid back.

"She went out of her mind afterward. She was guilt-ridden, blamed herself. I never made much sense to her constant ramblings until now."

"I find it hard to believe, but I've made my peace with her. I am going to win. I won't allow her to occupy any more of my thoughts or energy. I wanted to make both of you pay so much over the years. Pay for all my pain and lost childhood."

"Trenton, I'm so sorry. I wish I had known. I don't even know what to say. I can't imagine what you went through. But you survived and you're here."

"Yeah, here without the one thing that truly matters finally in my life." Bitterness filled the room. "I was wrong to let Jayla think I was you, but I couldn't help myself."

"It's okay. She's upset, but in time she may end up hearing your side of it. Give her a little space. She was questioning me about conversations the two of you have had and places you've been. I think I was able to convey to her that it was truly you she fell in love with."

Trenton laughed. "Love? I don't think so."

"Why not? What did you feel?"

Trenton stared at his hands. "I thought I loved her, but I don't know. Love isn't something I have experienced a lot of in my life."

Trenton looked up as Tristan moved to his side. "I'm glad you're here. It will take some time, I know, for you to feel trust, but I *want* you here. Know that." Tristan held out his hand for Trenton to shake.

Trenton stood. He shook Tristan's hand and pulled him close for a quick hug. "I'm glad I'm here, too. Give me some time to process things you've said about Mother tonight. We have very different views of who she really was. It's not going to be easy. I was hell-bent on ruining your life, you know."

"Yes, I noticed. The smoke bomb in the kitchen sink was a nice touch, by the way. So what made you change your mind, or should I say, *who?*" Tristan smiled.

"Yeah, get out of here, will ya? I need to sleep off this headache."

"Okay. But breakfast in the dining room tomorrow. And feel free to use the door instead of the secret passage." Tristan let himself out.

thirty-three

Trenton opened his eyes to the sun streaming through the bedroom window. For the first time in years, he had peace upon awakening. The pounding in his head was gone. He mulled over the conversation he had with Tristan. It was a start.

Jayla had changed his thinking. He craved the truth about his family more than ever right now, but he wanted her by his side as he reconciled with Tristan. He wanted her to be there while he learned what had really happened.

He sat up, placed his feet on the floor, and sighed. He didn't even know if Jayla would see him, but he could bet that she would be having coffee. He smiled as he thought of her ritual of closing her eyes and smelling it before starting to drink.

He showered in record time; anticipation quickened his morning ritual. He started toward the secret passage and stopped. He was no longer a stranger there and could use the front door.

With one last look in the mirror, he headed for the main house. Trenton entered the foyer, taking in every detail. Nothing had really changed since he was a child, and although he had wandered around at night, there was something different about reacquainting himself with the house in daylight.

He smelled fresh pastries, and his stomach rumbled, reminding him he hadn't eaten except the few bites at breakfast the day before. He moved in the direction of the dining room.

It was empty. Disappointed, he went to the sideboard and filled a mug with coffee, then placed a cheese Danish on his plate. His favorite table was still in the corner where he could watch the ocean and the door for Jayla.

He leaned back in the chair with his eyes closed and inhaled the strong aroma of coffee. His taste buds came alive with the scent, and he took a long sip, letting the moment warm him to his core. Outside the window, the waves rolled toward the rocks below.

"Looks like someone enjoys their coffee as much as my sister."

MIRRORED DECEPTION

Trenton looked up to see the spitting image of Jayla standing in front of him, with the exception of the cup of tea, as evident by the herbal scent, in her hand.

"You must be Jenna. I guess we didn't get properly introduced yesterday." Trenton stood and held out his hand, grasping hers firmly. "Please join me, unless you would rather not."

"I would love to." She took the seat across from him at the table as he lowered back down into his own chair.

"I'm sorry about the way we showed up yesterday," Jenna went on. "I'd been searching for Jayla for weeks. I was frantic and had no idea that she would just be off enjoying herself, while refusing to call her *loving* sister." She cast a kind smile.

"I understand." Trenton sipped his coffee. "Though I must admit it threw a wrench in my coming clean with Jayla. She must be pretty ticked at me right now."

"She is." Jenna met Trenton's eyes, and he saw warmth that encouraged him.

"So, *you're* not as ticked, I take it."

Jenna eyed him for a moment, then took a long drink of her tea. "I have no reason to be mad at you, other than you hurt my sister. I don't know you, Trent, but if you're anything at all like your brother, you had good intentions."

"I don't believe Jayla thinks that way."

"Give her some time. You have to see it was a shock for her." Jenna set down her cup and leaned forward. "I don't know what your reasons were, but I have a feeling it had a lot to do with your childhood. Yes, I was with Tristan when we found the diary. I'm so sorry, Trent, for all you went through. No child deserves that."

"Thanks. Not sure right now I even know who I am. The hatred that kept me going is gone, and now I just feel... *empty*.'"

Jenna reached a hand across the table and covered his. "Give it some time. Give yourself a chance to heal."

Jayla finished packing her bags. The night before, she'd told Jenna she was ready to go home. She moved to the window and watched the ocean. Part of her wanted to rent the cottage, but she couldn't risk running into Trenton anytime soon.

She threw the strap of her laptop bag over her shoulder, grabbed her other bag, and headed for the door. As she came down the stairs, the foyer was empty. She decided to put her bags in the car, and then get a coffee for the road.

She stopped short on the veranda. Trenton's bike was parked not far from her car. That meant he was close by. Her stomach clenched in anticipation of seeing him, and she scolded herself mentally for still wanting him after all he had done, or *not done* to her.

Why couldn't he just have been honest with me?

Had she really been completely honest with *him*?

MIRRORED DECEPTION

With the bags in the car, she turned and stared at the west wing. He had hidden there all that time and played with her like she was a toy. She had no idea when she'd interacted with Tristan or *Trenton*.

With a sigh, she moved toward the main entrance. Coffee would soothe her nerves.

She paused inside the door to the dining room and backed up slowly. Trenton was sitting at her favorite table with her sister.

Jayla turned and fled. She would not see him right now. If she went straight to the car, she could text Jenna and explain that she had already left for home. With a conscious effort, Jayla put Trenton from her mind and concentrated only on getting on the road.

She started her car, then reached for her phone. She typed in, *Can't see T right now. Stay as long as you like. Will see you at home.* and pushed *Send*.

She backed up to turn around and started down the driveway. With one eye on the rearview mirror, she watched the house disappear from sight. At the end of the driveway, she hesitated but a brief second before turning toward home. It was time to clean up the mess that had been left behind.

Jenna's phone vibrated in her pocket. She knew before she read it that Jayla had fled again.

"She's gone, isn't she?" Trent asked as Jenna slipped the phone back into her pocket.

"Yes, I'm afraid she is. She's choosing to not see you at the moment. I'm sorry, Trent. Don't give up on her." She stood and placed a hand over his. "She's upset, understandably so. Hang in there."

She turned and strode out of the dining room. Once the door shut, she moved to the side of the veranda and pulled out her phone. She read the text again and simply replied, *I'll see you when I get home.*

thirty-four

The past few days, Tristan had given Trenton space, only making small-talk when they ran into each other. Hopefully, today would be better.

Tristan walked down the stairs to find his brother at the front desk. He was just sitting there, papers in front of him, but not looking at them.

"Everything okay, Trent?"

"Yeah, I was just thinking we should start going over this stuff, if your offer for me to help out is still good?"

"Of course, it is. Let's bring the file into the dining room and have some coffee."

They spent the next hour going through the budget and profit sheets. Trenton was quick with the figures and Tristan was impressed, given his lack of formal education.

"I wanted to talk to you." Trenton paused and finished off his coffee. "For a long time now, I've wanted to get my GED."

Tristan sat back in his chair. "What's stopping you?"

"I don't know how to go about it, or what I need to do to prepare." His dark eyes pierced Tristan's. His eyes were no longer filled with anger, though they were intense and hard to read at times.

"Okay. There are books at the library to help you study, or online prep classes with tests. When you feel prepared, we'll get you signed up to take it." Tristan stood. "More coffee?"

"Yeah."

Tristan grabbed both mugs and went to the sideboard to fill them. He had been careful about things he said to his brother, but questions ran wild through his mind.

He handed the full mug to Trenton and slid into his chair. "I really need to know, Trenton, what it was like. Can we talk about this yet?"

"What *what* was like? My captive state? My mental anguish?" There was no bitterness in his voice, just flatness.

"I don't know, honestly. I just want to know everything that happened. I don't understand how the man we knew could have done that to you."

"The man we knew wasn't the man he was. Sam was an evil man, Tristan. I know you adored him. I did on some level, too, which is why I thought, in my childlike faith, that I could confront him about Dad and everything would just be made right. I knew it wouldn't bring Dad back. But to see him push our father off the cliff…I had nightmares about it for years." He sipped his coffee as Tristan sat waiting patiently for him to continue.

"It's not an easy thing to try and explain to you. Part of me wants to bury that time of my life forever and never think of it again, but on another level, I know I need to talk about it and get it out."

"You don't have to talk about it now. Only when you're ready." Tristan's voice trembled with emotion.

"I've spent years wishing I had the life you did. The life I should have had. You don't know what it's like to not go to school, to live in a pigsty, chained down until he came with slop for me to eat." He controlled his anger. "I can't forget it, though. I dream about it every night like it was yesterday."

"I'm sorry," Tristan whispered. "I wish I could turn back the clock and change everything."

"I wish I had been dead." The flatness of Trenton's voice spoke volumes. He stood. "Let's go over this stuff another time."

Before Tristan could say a word, he was gone. Tristan sat there staring at the empty doorframe Trenton had just passed through. His heart ached with sorrow at what his brother must have experienced, yet not being able to fathom or understand it completely. He knew he never would. Trenton needed to deal with it, and Tristan had no idea how to help him do that. They both would need professional help to get through this one.

He shuffled papers together, deciding he would just stick them in a folder and find Trent to go over them later. He wanted Trent to jump right into helping run the business, but he had doubts that his brother was ready for it. They both were on an emotional rollercoaster.

"I see it in your face." Jenna laid a hand on his arm. He hadn't heard her come in.

"What is it you see?"

"Frustration, anguish." Jenna slid into the chair. "You can't push him to talk about it. He will when he's ready. I wish Jayla was here – and talking to him."

"You and me both. He's lost without her."

Tristan stood, looking down at Jenna, and reached for her hand. "How about a walk?"

They strolled toward the cliff. The ocean turned, matching the sky, a dull gray. A storm was coming.

It fits Trenton. He needs to let his storm rage out, and then it will be calm.

Would it though? Would it ever be calm?

Trenton watched Tristan and Jenna from the window of the west wing. They seemed right together. He could see the way they looked at each other. He had felt that with Jayla.

His heart ached. He'd tried to call her, but she hadn't returned the calls.

He turned away from the window. How could he ever win her back? Without her by his side, he didn't want the life that he had so desperately wanted to be a part of

The headaches were getting worse, and he had no more excuses to put off getting them checked out. Maybe the focus he needed to have now was his health, rather than Jayla. He'd give her the space she obviously was going to make sure she had.

thirty-five

Jenna hung up the phone. She talked regularly with Jayla now. Although a part of her wanted to get home to spend time with her sister, Jenna hung on to every excuse she could find to stay put. She had great access to new antique places, which was business-related. Then, there was Tristan. The connection she felt with him was a force she had never reckoned with before.

She wished Jayla would give Trenton a chance. She had gotten to know him quite a bit in the past week since Jayla had left. He had a good heart, and now without the anger eating at him, was sincerely sorry for the trouble he had tried to cause Tristan's business for selfish gain. In the past weeks, Trenton had been getting help for his headaches and studying hard for his GED.

Jayla would have been proud of him. Every time Jenna brought him up in conversations, Jayla made it clear it was a subject she wasn't about to discuss with Jenna. Jenna smiled. She could be stubborn.

Jenna headed downstairs to look for Tristan—which had become her afternoon routine. They had started walking together every day. She couldn't imagine a day without having him by her side. Was that what Jayla had felt with Trenton?

"And there she is." Tristan was waiting at the bottom of the stairs. "Is Jayla okay?"

"She's good. Talked about finishing the book. She's going to take a hiatus from work for the year and just write."

They strolled hand and hand down the driveway. "She still won't discuss Trent at all."

"He hasn't mentioned her lately. I wondered if he gave up."

"I hope he's just giving her some time." Jenna sighed. "Why can't life be simple?"

"You want simple?"

"Absolutely."

"How about making it simple and move here?" Tristan glanced at her.

"Live here? You'd have one less room to rent."

"Maybe for a little while. I'm hoping you being a renter is a temporary status." He stopped and turned toward her. "Jenna, I'm crazy about you, and I want to see where our relationship will go beyond a summer fling."

"I feel the same. But Jayla—"

"No. Don't do that again. Jayla has made her choices and you need to support them and think of your own life. Moving here will not change anything for you and Jayla. You both need to support one another's choices." He held on to both of her hands. "Jenna, what does your heart tell you to do?"

She gazed into his eyes. "I want to be here with you. I can work from here just as easy, but it's not that simple."

"Why?" Tristan turned and started walking again.

She kept in step with him. "This has been so fast. I just don't know."

"Fast, yes, but we're not talking about getting married next week. We're talking about seeing where it goes. We're not even talking about really moving in with each other. We would have our own space, and we'll take it slow."

They walked in silence. Jenna's mind raced with possibilities. She wanted to agree to it without hesitation, but something held her back. She couldn't put her finger on it.

"You don't have to answer right now. I just ask that you think about it."

"I will." Jenna smiled up at him.

They continued without speaking. Jenna mentally made her pros-and-cons list that she had become painfully aware that she did for everything. There was no reason for her not to move. Jayla would want her to be happy and Tristan was right, it was time for Jenna to stop hovering over her sister.

"Are you sure this is what you want to do?" Jenna asked as they approached the driveway.

"I'm positive. I don't want to pressure you, though."

"You're not pressuring me. I've been thinking a lot about it before you even mentioned it. There has just been so much change in a short time, between Jayla and me—positive changes, healthy ones." Jenna chewed her bottom lip in concentration. "I'll do it."

Tristan grabbed her and spun her around in his arms. "Good."

"What about Trent? Will he be upset?"

"He has no reason to be, but if it makes you feel better, I'll talk to him about it."

thirty-six

Jayla sat in silence, listening to Jenna gush on about moving to The Cliffhouse to be near Tristan. Her stomach clenched at the longing to hear about Trenton. She couldn't forget him. He was in her thoughts during the day, her dreams at night.

"Did you hear me?" Jenna's voice broke through her thoughts.

"Yeah. That's great. I'm happy for you, Jen."

A soft sigh came across the line. "Jay, I know you miss him."

Jayla stood and paced the floor. "Yes, but it doesn't outweigh the lies."

"Can you honestly say you're ready to let go of those feelings? People aren't perfect, Jay. You can't just write him off without talking to him."

"Are you telling me you're okay with the lies he told?" Jayla stopped at the living room window and looked out across the parking lot of her apartment complex. She missed the ocean and the peace that consumed her with each rolling wave.

"No, it's not okay. But I think you should give him a chance to explain. You don't know what he's gone through."

"Sounds like you're condoning his behavior."

"I'm not! Jayla, whether you want to believe it or not, I think Trenton fell in love with you. I know he was planning on telling you everything before Tristan and I showed up." Jenna huffed. "When did you get so hard-hearted?"

"When the man I fell in love with turned out to be someone I didn't even know." Jayla bit her lip. "Jen, I can't talk about this with you. You're spending time with him, and who knows what lies he's filling your head with? I need to get on with my life."

"The sad fact of the matter is that you're *not* getting on with your life. I know you. You are sitting in that apartment thinking about him constantly. Give him a chance."

"I'll think about it, okay? Will that stop this conversation?" Jayla sank into the couch. "Listen, we'll talk later. I'll help you pack up your stuff if you want, but I won't go to The Cliffhouse to help you move." She quietly hung up the phone before Jenna had a chance to respond.

Jayla lay back on the couch and closed her eyes. Her stomach rumbled. Her nerves were wreaking havoc on her digestive system. She was nauseous and just plain sick over thinking of the lies Trent had told her.

Trenton's motorcycle hugged the curves as he cruised toward home. *Home.* It seemed so strange to call it that after so many years. The last few weeks had seemed like a lifetime. He was starting to trust Tristan and really beginning to believe his brother was telling the truth about his perspective on their strange family saga all those years.

Aware of his surroundings, he realized he had completely been lost in his thoughts and was already at The Cliffhouse. He parked the motorcycle and had just started for the west wing when he saw Tristan come down the stairs of the veranda.

"Hey, where've you been?"

"At the doctor, about the headaches."

"What'd you find out?" Tristan stopped short, his eyes scanning over Trenton.

"Don't worry, I'm not going to keel over anytime soon." Trent switched his helmet to the other hand. "Come on and I'll tell you about it, if you have time."

"I have time. I was actually coming to talk to you."

They moved toward the west wing in silence. Trenton pushed open the door and walked inside. He slid his helmet onto a table and turned to Tristan. "What did you want to talk about?"

"It can wait. I think your appointment is probably more important."

Trenton gestured toward the living room and followed after Tristan when he headed that way. Settling onto the couch, while Tristan took a chair, Trenton looked around. The place still had such memories. Maybe it wasn't the place Trent should be living, at least for the time being.

He realized Tristan was waiting for him, so he focused on his brother. "Well, I have what they call PTSD, or posttraumatic stress disorder. It's the aftermath of a traumatic event or series of events." He took a deep breath.

"What do they do for it, and what about the headaches?" Tristan sat forward in the chair.

"Well, it manifests itself in many ways. Basically, I need to learn how to understand and control cutting myself off. There are techniques to learn to help me stay in the present, not regress into the abusive and traumatic past. Learning to tolerate day-to-day life without anxiety or flashbacks." He sighed. "All sounds so fun, doesn't it?"

"It's not going to be easy. What can I do to help?"

Maybe they had come full circle after all. "I'm going to be looking for a therapist to help deal with the stress and flashbacks, coping with that should, in turn, lessen the headaches." He eased forward on the couch. "Would you be willing to go with me a few times?"

"Of course. I think it would be helpful for both of us."

"Good. Maybe then, after getting a grip a bit better, I can figure out how to get Jayla to talk to me."

They sat silently, each engrossed in their own thoughts.

"That's part of what I wanted to talk to you about." Tristan broke the quiet.

"Jayla?"

"Sort of. More like Jenna. I asked her to move here, so we can be together and see where our relationship goes. Are you okay with that?"

"Does it matter?"

"Yes. If you feel very strongly that you don't want her around because she reminds you of Jayla, I certainly will accept that, and Jenna and I will figure something else out."

"Really, Tristan, you would put your life on hold for your long-lost brother?" Trenton struggled to contain his amusement.

"Why not?"

"Because you'd be a bigger fool than I am if you did that. I don't have a problem with it. I'm thinking that staying here in the west wing isn't such a good idea, though. Too many memories of Sam here."

"Where are you going?"

"Not far. I had offered the cottage to Jayla and cleaned it for her. I'm thinking I'll go stay there. Close enough to help out around here, but far enough away from the bad memories."

Tristan slowly nodded. "Okay. We could look into remodeling the west wing and making more rooms for the bed-and-breakfast."

"Or, you could remodel it as a home for you. You need to start planning your future, Bro," Trenton said. "Don't let The Cliffhouse run your life, Tristan. Life's too short."

Trenton stood up. "Now get out of here, so I can do what I need to about moving to the cottage."

thirty-seven

Jayla packed up the last box. She had found a new apartment. It had been four months since her adventure over the summer, and she still thought of Trenton.

A soft knock at the door drew her attention. She pushed the box aside, went to the door, and opened it. She gasped when she saw him standing there, motorcycle helmet in hand, leaning against the doorframe.

"I know you probably still don't want to see me,

but I need to talk to you."

Jayla stepped back, gesturing him in.

"Jayla, I've missed you."

"Trenton, I'm not sure what you want me to say. I'm not even sure who you are." She sat on the couch and curled her legs under her.

Trenton joined her and faced her square on. "Jayla, it's me. You know me, and you *knew* me. It was me you got to know. I pretended to be Tristan, but it was me on the motorcycle, me making love to you that night."

"Trenton, if you felt we were close enough to make love, why didn't you tell me? Was it just casual sex?"

"No. I was falling in love with you. I wanted to tell you so bad, but I was afraid I would lose you forever."

"I would have rather heard it from you than come face to face with Tristan thinking I was with him."

"Yeah, I see where that is a bit disconcerting. So much from my past affected my judgment. I wasn't making good decisions at all. In the past few months, Tristan and I have had a chance to really talk and begin to understand each other. We both have learned so much about our past that we never knew. We've been attending therapy to deal with the past and my childhood, or lack thereof." Trenton ran his fingers through his hair. "I came here to say I'm sorry. Jayla, I love you. I want to try and make this up to you somehow."

"You don't know what has changed in the last few months."

MIRRORED DECEPTION

"How bad can it be compared to my past?" Trenton smiled. "I'm sure we can handle anything. Give us a chance."

"I don't know."

"Would it help if I tell you that Tristan and Jenna know I'm here and are rooting for us?"

"That's not fair." Jayla hugged her arms around herself. "I'm moving. I have a new apartment. I took a year off work."

"Yes, I know. Jenna told me. She also said you're trying to publish your book. I think that's great. What else, Jayla?"

She stood up and paced the floor. "Things are different now. We knew each other only a few weeks, and I'm not in the habit of sleeping with men that quickly."

"Okay. We rushed in a little bit." Trenton stood and pulled her close. He nibbled at her earlobe, and a sigh escaped her. "Tell me you want me to go, and I will." He smiled.

"Not fair, Trenton. I need to tell you something."

"Okay, tell me." He kissed the curve of her neck, then onto her shoulder, and she shivered.

Jayla pushed him away. "Trenton, stop. You're not listening. This is the exact reason I'm trying to tell you this now."

"What? Tell me what?"

"I'm pregnant."

Trenton stared at her. Slowly, the corners of his lips turned up and twitched. "Do you think it will be twins?"

"Oh, Lord, help us."

He drew her against him. "I know it's soon, but marry me. I love you, Jayla. Let me be a husband to you, a father to our child, or children if we are that blessed. Marry me."

She searched his eyes. She'd never seen him so alive and full of love. She was scared, and yet, she had never had such confidence in herself as the time she had been with him. He was her other half.

"Yes, heaven help me, yes." She kissed him to seal her vow, then slid her fingers into his hair and pulled him close.

Finally, she knew exactly who he was, and who *she* was in this crazy world.

Enjoy a sample chapter of
TRUSTING LOVE
BY EMMA LEIGH REED

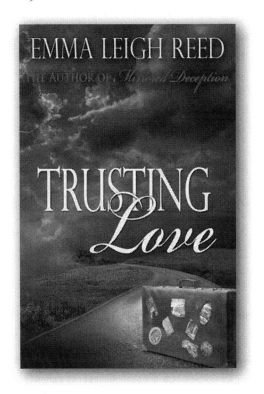

CHAPTER ONE

Chloe Wilder shot up in bed. She rubbed her eyes with the back of her hands trying to adjust to the dim moonlight that filtered in through the closed blinds. Her heart raced as she took in the shadows that danced around the room. She swiped her hand across her face to wipe away the tears the nightmare left behind. Wrapping her arms around her knees, she hugged herself tight.

This same nightmare had become recurrent. Her arms wrapped around her waist, she whispered, "I won't let anything happen to you."

She pushed the covers off, jumped out of bed, and crossed to the window. It was dark except for the light of the moon. No street lights were lit. There was no better time than now.

She pulled on an old pair of sweat pants and a baggy sweater. She dragged an old tattered suitcase from the closet and started packing. A sense of urgency came upon her as she shoved in the last shirt and closed the suitcase. She glanced around the room and her eyes stopped on a picture of her parents. They held each other, smiling. It was obviously taken at a happy moment. She picked up the picture and looked closer. Sadness and shame overwhelmed her. Holding it close, Chloe closed her eyes and prayed for forgiveness for the mistakes she had made in her life. Putting the picture in her purse, she picked up the suitcase and slipped through the door into the night.

She threw the old suitcase in the backseat of her beloved Toyota. The vehicle was on its last leg, but somehow it kept running. Chloe prayed it would take her far away from this town, and even further from all the pain. She needed a fresh start for her and her baby she vowed to protect.

She drove with her lights on low, praying no one would see her. Turning onto a back road she blew out a sigh of relief as the road lead her out of town. Time was of the essence. She had a small window of opportunity to put distance between Tony and her. Chloe didn't know what had possessed her to get involved with him. He had been quite a charmer in the beginning. Now thoughts of Tony brought only regret and fear. She shuddered at the thought of what he would do when he found her gone.

The night seemed to get blacker as she drove further out of town. Tension knotted her neck and her arms ached from gripping the steering wheel. Chloe forced out a deep breath and turned the radio to a soft rock station. She allowed herself to relax just a fraction after driving for hours into the night.

Miles passed. The sky turned from black to a gray with a tinge of pink in the horizon. Chloe's eyes grew heavy. She found a rest area facing the ocean and pulled in. Locking her doors, she closed her eyes. *Just a few minutes of sleep, then I will keep moving.*

The house was quiet when Tony slipped inside. He smirked in the dark. Chloe was so predictable—always in bed before he got home hoping to avoid him. He could see through her, but she was easily influenced and good to have around. He made his way to the kitchen to grab a beer. Twisting off the cap, he slipped into living room and sat down. His legs sprawled in front of him he lounged back in the easy chair.

Chloe had been young when he had found her. She was eager for love and he gave it to her. Well, maybe not the love she had been looking for, but he didn't care what she needed. He did feel sorry when he saw her tears but now he's bored and ready to move on, but can't. She overhead too many conversations and knew too much.

He sighed and placed the empty bottle on the table next to him, stood and started upstairs. Something had to be done with her. He slipped into the bathroom off the bedroom and turned on the light. Tony expected to see Chloe huddled on the edge of the bed. He did a double take when he realized the bed was empty.

What the hell. He flipped on the bedroom light. She had been there. The covers were tossed aside. He pulled open a bureau drawer. Her clothes were gone. His fists clenched at his sides as he raced downstairs.

He pulled his cell phone from his pocket and punched in a number.

"She's gone… I don't know where, just find her and fast…" He disconnected, picked up the empty beer bottle and flung it against the wall. The glass shattered into tiny pieces that sprayed across the hard wood floor. "Chloe, what have you done?"

ABOUT THE AUTHOR

EMMA LEIGH REED, originally from New Hampshire, now resides in Tennessee. She has fond memories of the Maine coastline and incorporates the ocean into all her books. She has three grown children and is enjoying her empty nest. Her life has been touched and changed by her son's autism - she views life through a very different lens than before he was born. Growing up as an avid reader, it was only natural for Emma Leigh to turn to creating the stories for others to enjoy. Emma Leigh continues to learn through her children's strength and abilities that pushes her to go outside her comfort zone on a regular basis. She is the author of romantic suspense, women's fiction and has co-authored children's books.

emmaleighreed.com

ALSO AVAILABLE FROM
EMMA LEIGH REED

ALSO AVAILABLE FROM
EMMA LEIGH REED

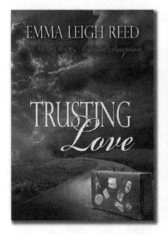

ALSO AVAILABLE FROM
E. L. REED

Made in the USA
Columbia, SC
04 November 2022